The Ballet Lover

Barbara L. Baer

Open Books

Published by Open Books

Cover photo "Ballet Shoes" © by Kryziz Bonny
Learn more about the photographer at flickr.com/photos/kryziz/

ISBN-10: 0615722865 /ISBN-13: 978-0615722863

Contents

Acknowledgments

Part One

One

*In 1963, Frederick Ashton choreographed Marguerite and Armand for
Margot Fonteyn and the recent Soviet defector, Rudolf Nureyev. The
one-act ballet's sizzling sonata by Franz Liszt, libretto modeled after
Dumas fils novel La Dame Aux Camélias was the perfect vehicle for
aging Fonteyn. At the Covent Garden premiere, fans rained flowers
upon the stage and Ashton declared that no other pair would ever
dance Marguerite and Armand. "There was a sort of animality, as
there was a physical intensity and a sexual impulse that charged the
atmosphere with electricity."*

Geneva Robbins stood for a moment marveling at
the vaulted, golden dome of Covent Garden, then
slipped into the middle of a deserted row in the orchestra
section. "No press at rehearsals, so be invisible," Connor
told her. "That won't be hard for you, my little brown
hen with a flaming pen. Get us something juicy."

When the uniformed usher was looking the other
way, Geneva took her small notebook and penlight
from her purse. Scrunched deep into her velvet seat,
she wouldn't be noticed among the glitterati of Rudolf

Nureyev's international clique, come from near and far to see Natalia Makarova and Rudolf Nureyev's get-acquainted rehearsal for *Romeo and Juliet* with the Royal Ballet. These fans spoke loudly and dramatically in French which Geneva understood, German and Russian which she identified only words and emphasis on certain syllables. Loudest of all was Madame Veliani, the Egyptian heiress married to an oil Texan, blood-red hair massed on her shoulders. Geneva had seen the woman with Nureyev at the Tea Room and had been similarly repulsed by her. In an eardrum piercing voice, Veliani ticked off Nureyev's superhuman schedule of performances. "Athens, Melbourne, Johannesburg. Only the North Pole, he's not danced there. Now he runs himself to the ground to come to London for this minor Russian. Really, he shouldn't strain himself the way he does."

Natalia Makarova a minor Russian? Geneva clenched her pen. Makarova was the most exciting ballerina to emerge from the Kirov for a generation. She was a perfect stylist with dramatic intensity. The strident *parti pris* for Nureyev wasn't the first Geneva had heard of a strain, a conflict, between the Russian defectors. Audiences loved the way Nureyev's ardent youth and erotic power transformed fiftyish Fonteyn into a tremulous girl, especially English fans who revered Fonteyn and saw Makarova an interloper.

The Royal Ballet's *corps*, dressed in velvet and doublets for the opening ball, was warming up at the back of the stage. A short, muscular boy in a green tunic and harlequin hose made Geneva grin. The British always found wonderful small men as character dancers, natural-born Pucks and Ariels.

Stately Georgina Parkinson, the ballet mistress for the rehearsal, came onstage wearing the robes of a noble lady of Verona. *Queen mothers, the fate of the ageing ballerina,* Geneva wrote quickly. But it was a pleasure to see a mature figure among too many girls Geneva thought looked as starved of emotion as they were of nourishment.

Nureyev emerged in baggy leg-warmers, doffed his fisherman's cap to the audience and walked on tip toes to the back as if to surprise the boy in green. There, the object of all eyes, he played with little Puck, stretch for stretch, deep bend for deep bend, sweeping his arms back and over his head. Unlike the boy who worked in silence, Nureyev grunted and groaned. Madame Veliani called out, "Poor Rudi, don't hurt yourself." Geneva wrote, *His Highness' arrogance.*

Individual instruments in the orchestra pit tuned up, the violin coming forward with Juliet's poignant theme. Nureyev lifted his nose and widened his nostrils as if smelling the Russian steppes. Vera Volkova, another grande dame responsible for transmitting Russian ballet traditions, was supposed to have told Fonteyn that Nureyev didn't have a nose. "He has nostrils." Nureyev was an aphrodisiac to men and women, but Geneva felt too annoyed at his clique and his preening, as well as his history of mistreating ballerinas, to join that infatuated company.

Natalia Makarova entered from the wings in pink toe shoes that squeaked newness. She wore a tulle skirt too wide for her delicate body, and a disaster of a golden wig, a foot of faux Renaissance curls that made her strain to keep up her small head.

Nureyev clapped his hand to his mouth in mock fright at the wig as if he were seeing Gorgon's writhing locks. Makarova shielded her eyes like a shy child. In this moment, Geneva felt the prima ballerina was in danger of giving away her authority. She seemed all nerves when she missed picking up a step. Was she confusing the Soviet version of the ballet with the British choreography? Geneva had only seen the Bolshoi Ballet's production of *Romeo and Juliet* on film at the Lincoln Center Dance Library, Leonid Lavrosky's original version that had premiered in Moscow in 1940, shortly before the German invasion of Russia. Galina Ulanova as Juliet and Konstantin Sergeyev as Romeo danced the Soviet heroic-style choreography as proud lovers in desperate times.

Geneva remembered a story that Makarova told her in their interview a month earlier in New York. The ballerina recounted how she often experimented with her thin pale hair to make it look darker and thicker. In 1961, her first time in Paris, she bought a color dye. In her room, she couldn't read the instructions in French, and left the treatment on so long that it singed off most of her hair. "I have only baby hair. Awful. I look awful," she told Geneva. Some days later, as the Kirov troupe waited at Le Bourget airport to board their plane for London, Nureyev made his famous asylum-leap into the arms of French police. In the turmoil, the company minders rushed them all to the plane. En route to London, the Kirov directors scrambled to recast all the ballets Nureyev had been scheduled to dance. Makarova wasn't to have danced *Giselle*—she was not Nureyev's partner— but now they called her from her seat to tell her she was chosen to open the company's London tour.

In London, a wardrobe mistress found a peasant-girl dress that fit, and to cover the ballerina's singed hair, they gave her a hideous wig, perhaps this same one.

"So ugly," Makarova remembered, "I thought I die, really." Despite her fears, she became the surprise star of the season and saved face for her country and the Kirov.

Now, with an intake of breath, the ballerina extended her long forearms upward in Juliet's beautiful signature arabesque, lifting herself into attitude, every cell yearning for Romeo. But she must have held her pose too long because rather than float into his arms, she collided with Nureyev's back. Perhaps he turned away. Russian words followed.

Nureyev in his leg warmers now circled. He threw his hands in the air and stared out at the audience. Laughter erupted.

Geneva wrote with the tiny pen's light. *Crude people laugh. Worried for NM.*

When Makarova spun and missed her timing again, Nureyev stepped aside and almost let her fall, reaching out his hand at the last moment.

Geneva gasped, unbelieving. He was endangering his ballerina. Any fall could do damage, even break a bone or tear a tendon.

Geneva remembered Makarova's words in New York, "I am vulnerable."

Georgina Parkinson came out to talk with the dancers. She huddled beside Nureyev. Geneva hoped she was appealing to him to help Makarova learn her role, to stress how his countrywoman depended on him. Nureyev scratched his head, waggled his hands at his side like Petrushka and assumed his innocent *I didn't do anything* pose. Georgina walked to where Makarova was staring at her feet. She nodded her small head beneath the ominous wig. "Da, Da," Geneva heard her say.

Under Parkinson's gaze, Nureyev showed Makarova where she should place herself for lifts, where she must land. She still seemed tentative when they began the adagio, their last embrace before Romeo's flight to Padua. Geneva held her breath. Makarova stumbled. Nureyev expelled the word "idiot" loudly, Russian intonation on the final syllable. Georgina Parkinson held up her hand. "Ladies and gentleman, break here. Everyone back in half an hour and we'll go through to the end."

Nureyev sprang into the orchestra pit where he greeted friends and kissed the painted cheeks of Madame Veliani who whispered in his ear and made him bray. A fat man with mutton chops and suspenders popped a champagne bottle close enough to send fizz into Geneva's face. He handed a glass to Nureyev who drained it.

Geneva was keeping her head down, writing and trying not to be observed, when she realized the chatter around her had stopped. She raised her eyes to see Nureyev with his hands on his hips at the end of her row, staring in her direction. She pulled back her head to give him an unobstructed view of the young man in the row, assuming he was the object of interest. Connor had described Nureyev's penchant for quickies between the acts, how sex didn't deplete but rather invigorated Rudi.

"Come, we go to talk." Nureyev was crooking his finger at Geneva and no one else. Had he seen her taking notes? Was he going to humiliate her for thinking subversive thoughts? He kept beckoning. She had no choice but to obey. She rose, knees trembling, apologized for stepping over legs to get to the aisle while she felt eyes burning into the back of her head. It occurred to her that Nureyev might remember Connor introducing them at the Russian Tea Room, and that he mistook her for an important person.

As she followed Nureyev up the aisle, Geneva remembered the first time she'd been invited to the Tea Room, and that evening Nureyev had made his appearance. Stepping into the dark Tea Room had seemed like entering the theater in the reverent moments before the lights came up and the show began. Slowly, as her eyes and ears adjusted to the dim hush, the tables illumined by glowing lamps, the silhouettes of women in smart hats with feathers and smoke rising from cigarette holders in the red banquette seats, came into focus.

"What is your choice in caviar, black or red?" Connor asked Ruth.

"Black always best," said Ruth.

"Two orders of black Beluga, three naked vodkas with a twist of lemon," he told the young blond waiter with a wispy beard. "And bring a bottle of bubbly on ice. We don't want to go thirsty." He took Ruth's hand.

"Auntie is trés chic," Connor whispered to Geneva. "I like rouge on a woman. A dab of color wouldn't hurt you, child." His finger brushed her cheek and Geneva blushed. Thank heavens her Aunt Ruth was there for moral support because she was tongue-tied, so unused to having her appearance noticed. Ruth, however, appeared entirely concentrated on the caviar. She slathered butter on a piece of toast, dug her spoon into the pot with shiny black eggs, and popped it in her mouth, closing her eyes to chew. Ruth wiped her lips daintily and reached for another toast.

"And where in Russia did you call home?" Connor asked.

"I didn't say Russian." Ruth held out her cigarette for him to light.

"My aunt spent involuntary time in far eastern Russia, but she's Polish, like her sister, who managed to escape to Geneva, Switzerland where I was born," said Geneva.

"So that explains your name," said Connor. "Don't remove further veils of mystery all at once. Russia is mystery, Poland not so much. Switzerland—all cheese."

Suddenly Connor picked up his napkin to fan himself. "We are in *luck* tonight."

"The fish comes?" asked Ruth, who had ordered the expensive sturgeon with new potatoes and cabbage in a sour cream sauce.

"Don't turn around yet. God's son just descended to earth." Connor brought the back of his hand to his neck, tipped back his chair. "Try not to show you're overcome."

Everyone in the room stopped talking, eating, and

drinking as Rudolf Nureyev, wearing doe-skin suede from his high boots to his jockey cap, walked forward, followed by a woman with a carmine head of hair and lobster-red mouth.

"Rudi!" Connor waggled his hand.

Nureyev leaned down, extended his index finger. Conner touched it for an instant, a gesture mimicking Michelangelo's "Father to Son." Connor then introduced Ruth and Geneva as Russian ballet friends. Nureyev greeted them in Russian and swept past.

"It's so atavistic, the power Rudi has. You can almost smell the primeval damp rising. My nose was shiny, wasn't it?"

Ruth dabbed Connor's forehead with a napkin. "Don't flatter Tatars, not cultured."

"That's perfectly true and why we're all in love with them," Connor said.

"Who was the violent-looking redheaded person?" Geneva asked.

Connor laughed. "Madame Mansari Veliani, when she's with Rudi, she won't allow anyone near without making a scene. She is fabulously wealthy and her husband is Texas oil. She's named a restaurant in Austin she calls Rudi's Ranch. Imagine what goes on there while they roast the beef balls?"

Geneva looked at her lap. Ruth probably hadn't understood and didn't laugh.

"You blush so easily, dear," Connor said to Geneva, again patting her hand.

"I didn't say anything," Geneva replied.

"Your expression says it all. I shocked you about the bull balls."

"Like her mother." Ruth waved her cigarette over the carpet. In a moment the young waiter was kneeling to sweep up ash. "Celia was very intelligent but not smart."

"I'm not like Celia in any way," answered Geneva.

When the check arrived, Ruth and Geneva tried not to notice the $100 bills Connor placed on the salver. The night's supper cost their combined weekly salaries.

"Let me see you ladies to your cab," said Connor.

"We walk. Good after such eating," Ruth said.

"You may have slogged across Siberia but tonight you will take a cab."

In the taxi, Ruth eased off her pumps and stretched her feet.

"We didn't go hungry. We ate good. In Yakutsk, I dream of fat man like Connor invites me to restaurant."

"If Connor knew you called him fat, there would be no more caviar or kisses on gloved fingertips." Geneva said.

"He likes boys," said Ruth.

"Why do you say that?" The blush returned to burn Geneva's cheeks.

Ruth patted Geneva's knee, opened her window and lit a cigarette.

———————

Nureyev's striding figure in baggy pants led up a dark stairway into a corridor where he stopped, produced a key to a door emblazoned with a royal crest, motioned

Geneva to step into a gold-brocaded box that opened onto the stage below.

"Here Queen sits. And here I am." Nureyev pointed to the seat with the royal crest and indicated Geneva take the chair behind it. He mimed writing in a notebook. Was he giving permission or ordering her to take notes?

"Once I dress as footman. Game I play with Queen who laughs like horse." He snorted, somehow softening his features until he looked uncannily like Elizabeth II. Connor had told her if Rudolf hadn't been a dancer, he'd have been a comic actor.

Nureyev's gold-green eyes speckled with mischief and the scar on his lip glistened. His sweater was damp and warm with perspiration and the wool had a musky earthy smell. This close, she felt her resistance drain away. She was cold and hot in different parts of her body at the same time.

The entire time alone with Nureyev, Geneva never opened her mouth to ask a question. How could she when Rudolf Nureyev talked non-stop. She didn't know how long she sat, or whether she accurately got down on paper anything he said. If she'd had a question, her voice wouldn't have come out louder than a squeak. Later, trying to transcribe, she remembered that every verb, every gesture that Nureyev used was in the present.

"Not so many years classical dancing left for me." He had looked at his feet in their pair of old grey dance slippers. "I use self up, burn self out, stretch body before I am finished. I want choreographer to squeeze me dry—like lemon." He squeezed his fist. "When I have no more juice, I am happy."

Nureyev lay down on the carpet two feet from Geneva to demonstrate a writhing motion. "For modern dance, I must relax back. Contract, not expand muscles, move into floor. You are tree or animal. You make knots, tie and untie self on floor." Then he got up and looked over the edge of the box to the stage below where Georgina Parkinson was teaching Makarova her steps for Juliet's visit to the Friar. At the moment that Makarova ran from side to side with the vial of the Friar's sleeping potion raised in her hands, Nureyev extended his arms over his head and gave a great yawn that made everyone below turn their heads toward him.

He bowed slightly to Geneva, doffed his cap, sprang two steps upward and out of the Royal Box, leaving Geneva alone to face Natalia Makarova's dark eyes.

By the time Geneva stumbled down the stairs to sit in the back of the orchestra, Makarova was lying in the family crypt in pretend-death from the friar's potion. Nureyev arrived, picked up a knife, and stabbed himself several times, rolling his eyes before falling on the stage. Makarova rose and walked stiff-legged into the wings.

Nureyev stripped off his leg warmers and began to unroll another layer from his waist until between his flesh-colored unitard and bulging dance belt there was little to imagine. Geneva heard him say, "Natasha, come. Time is money." He crooked his finger toward the wings. "Come, Natasha, let us work."

For the next hour, Nureyev rehearsed Makarova in *Romeo and Juliet*. He was gentle, even paternal, with his ballerina.

Two

In 1965, Kenneth MacMillan re-staged Romeo and Juliet for the Royal Ballet, using Sergei Prokofiev's score but transforming the choreography. Lynn Seymour and Christopher Gable were cast for the premiere, but at the last moment, recast the choreographer Margot Fonteyn and Rudolf Nureyev as the star-crossed lovers. Nureyev, a bandage wrap around an injured leg, wooed Fonteyn with such ardor that the audience would not let the dancers leave the stage. After 43 curtain calls, the safety curtain was lowered and the lights went out.

G eneva left the rehearsal as the sun dipped over the Thames. Despite the July warmth, she shivered as she walked along the river. She felt delayed shock, a numbing awareness that Nureyev had used her to betray Natalia Makarova. She could hear Connor's whisper. *Don't be stupid. You couldn't buy that time. Think thighs.* On the positive side, Nureyev and Makarova had completed rehearsal for tonight's performance.

She continued down the Embankment along the busy thoroughfare until she saw a row of costume shops. Connor must know these old theatrical haunts, she thought. She'd take a look, get her mind off the morning's drama. She pushed open the door and reeled back from the vapors of sweat and mildew. Before she could step back onto the street, a small, round woman with peroxide curls emerged from behind a rack and asked, "May I help you, dear? You want a theater suit. One your size just came in. You'll love it." Without waiting for Geneva's answer, the woman climbed up a step ladder with surprising agility, her muscled legs encased in mesh nylons. She backed down with a bag.

"This frock hasn't been hung out yet but I wager it's the very one Vivien Leigh wore in *Waterloo Bridge*, and will get snapped up in the minute I pull it out. My name's Viv, too. I wasn't always this size." She patted her hips. "Danced in the Follies in Paris."

Viv pulled a black silk suit with lapels and big shoulders from the bag. If it had arrived recently, not sometime decades ago, dust gathered quickly, Geneva thought.

"I don't need clothing. I'm just looking for souvenirs."

"Put yourself in it, luv. You'll fall in love."

Geneva stepped into the skirt and buttoned the jacket that hugged her torso in an astonishing way. The material gave her waist definition. Vivien Leigh I am not, Geneva said to herself. I have a snub nose, for one thing, and ginger hair that frizzes but this jacket does something for me.

The blond Vivien handed her high taffeta pumps and stockings with rhinestones with a black seam up the back. Geneva, who had one pair of heels she seldom wore, stared at their height. A veiled cloche was passed behind the dressing curtain.

"Try it all. Ten pounds for the lot."

"Shall I wear it out like this?" Geneva asked.

"Magic!" Vivian stepped back and clapped her hands. "Absolutely don't take a stitch off until someone does it for you."

Geneva couldn't help the blush, it just rose from somewhere in her clavicle upward. Viv was already stuffing her old clothes back inside the plastic bag. Geneva handed her ten pounds.

"Have a smashing evening, luv. Give my best to the dark prince."

Further down the street, Geneva passed an olive-skinned beauty standing in the doorway of Najiba's Salon. In a musical exotic voice, the willowy person in a red sari said, "I can do wonders for that hair, sweetie, to go with the gorgeous outfit."

In minutes, Geneva was seated, having her scalp scrubbed clean of tension. She stayed in Najiba's nearly two hours for a henna rinse, a post wash scalp massage, a blow-dry that straightened her frizz into a shiny fall of reddened hair. As she gave herself over to Najiba's expert hands and the scents of sandal that rose from her golden skin, Geneva let her mind wander, back to meeting Natalia Makarova a month earlier.

———————

Geneva and Ruth had been in the middle of Saturday apartment cleaning, with Ruth running the vacuum and Geneva scrubbing the sink when the phone rang.

Ruth answered, "Connor, you good?" In a minute,

she handed Geneva the phone.

"You have fifteen minutes to get to the Mayflower Hotel on Central Park West where Natasha Makarova is waiting for you to interview her."

"Natalia Makarova granted an interview? I'm not prepared for that."

"She's agreed to a special interview with *Icarus* and I'm sending you. Go forth," he said. "It's the perfect opportunity to unleash your talent for modesty."

As the cab sped downtown along the park, Geneva scribbled questions. Natalia Makarova said to interviewers that she'd defected entirely for art, for the freedom to dance a wider modern repertoire of ballets. Had this happened? That was her opening.

The cab arrived and Geneva stared up at the building, got out and paid.

At the door to Makarova's suite, Geneva cleared her throat. "Miss Makarova."

The answer came in husky English accented like Aunt Ruth's, "Come."

Drapery at the far end of a living room parted enough for a glimmer of the Park's foliage to seep in.

Geneva's first glimpse of the ballerina in repose made her think she was seeing a work of art, not a woman. The dancer, seated beside a reading lamp, wore her pale blond chignon pulled tightly back to the fastening of a high-necked dress. Makarova'a long neck—her nickname in school had been "the ibis"—canted forward.

As Geneva approached, the ballerina extended her fingers. Her long, pinkish opal fingernails seemed to reach out to touch Geneva's hand, but before that happened, the dancer inserted a gold-tipped cigarette in a long black holder and lit its tip. The sleeve of her dress, the fall of silky, clingy material in a burnished copper, glowed.

"What a beautiful dress," Geneva said. "The material and the color are so unusual, so classic. You look like a Vermeer."

Makarova smiled. Geneva had chosen the right words.

"When I defect, I leave everything. I have only one little bag in hand, clothes I am wearing. In London and New York, I buy completely new wardrobe. Thirty-year-old woman has such possibility starting life new. I buy silk, leather, fur."

"I saw you perform two extraordinary *Swan Lakes* in San Francisco recently. They were brilliant and different each performance—especially your Odile, who you made almost another woman from one night to the next."

"Yes, *Swan Lake*. Three years in West, I dance many old roles but none express me now. I must create now, Sol Hurok tells me, 'Natasha, you are destined to be international,' but now, after I wait for choreographer to use my talents."

Geneva noted: *frustration, roles.*

The dancer touched the hollow of her collar bone above her heart.

"*Giselle*. No more *Giselle*," Makarova sighed. Her heavy eyelids dark with a blue shadow drooped as if from their weight.

"*Giselle*, your signature ballet," said Geneva. "I heard

you once danced her thirteen times in a row."

Makarova exhaled smoke and sighed. "I leave Russia to dance modern works, but public pays to see *Giselle.* I try to make psychologically different all performances but sometimes I am so tired of stupid boring crazy girl."

Geneva remembered a strange *Giselle* she'd seen on tape where Makarova looked unbalanced long before Albrecht betrayed her.

"At American Ballet Theater," Geneva said, "you danced with Erik Bruhn in a modern piece. I believe it was *The Miraculous Mandarin.*"

"Yes, but modern ballets, some are interesting, some not so much. I am waiting for choreographer who understands what is here, inside me, for psychological character."

Geneva was sorry no photographer had been able to accompany her because the ballerina seemed to pass through transformations only a camera could capture. In that moment, her elbow and clavicle, cheek bones and nose, had the definition of a Medieval wood-cut. On stage, Natalia Makarova's extraordinary thinness made her appear weightless. Ballerinas starved themselves but there was more to the ethereal figure that Makarova projected than absence of flesh—it was as if her bones were lighter, air-filled like a bird's. Up close, seeing the dancer with a wreath of smoke rising around her, she seemed an icon in a vaporous halo, hardly more than a shimmering outline.

"I want to dance lonely people, what you call *eccentrics.* On tour with Kirov, I see *Persona,* Bergman film. I recognize myself in Liv Ullmann's face." She paused.

"You also know painter Gustave Moreau?" Before waiting for Geneva to answer, she continued. "In Paris, I see paintings of Ophelia and Sphinx. I see myself."

Geneva noted: *Gustave Moreau*, a name she didn't know.

Geneva pulled her chair closer. The ballerina's voice, already low and whispery as the faintest sliver of sound, was muffled by Makarova speaking more to herself than to her listener, an almost trancelike state of self-absorption, as if remembering something that she might lose. She also seemed unaware that ash was about to fall onto the carpet. Geneva extended a glass ashtray from the table and caught the ash as it was falling.

"I came to West where everyone can be individual. I regret nothing. I am fatalist by nature with strong belief in predestination." She raised her thin arms. "In summer 1969, I decide, I must go to West."

Makarova snubbed out her cigarette and placed another in its holder but didn't light it. "I am innocent in soul, like child. I make plans, but we have fate, don't you agree?" She raised and lowered her thin shoulders. "Modern woman, twentieth century woman is broken. In French, it is *fébrile*. What is English word?"

Geneva searched her mind. "*Fébrile*. I think it means something like delicate of spirit, highly strung, perhaps vulnerable to things."

Makarova smiled. "Ah, yes. I try to say in English I have vulnerability in life, on stage. I give myself like child when I trust. I take back when not trust."

Just then, the phone on the table rang and Makarova picked it up.

Geneva sat without moving, struck by the light of Central Park and the closeness to the ballerina who was frowning as she listened to voices on the line. Geneva looked at her notes. She hadn't asked much but she could retrieve a theme.

"Mama!" Makarova cried into the phone. Then aside to Geneva she said, "I must talk to Mother now. Forgive me."

"You've been generous with your time," Geneva replied.

"Spiritual frustration here as in Russia. Can woman of imagination ever be satisfied?" Makarova spoke over the mouthpiece, placing her hand on her forehead. "Yes, *da da,* Mama."

"Good bye, and thank you," Geneva backed out toward the door.

———————

When Geneva entered the dark Tea Room to meet Connor after the interview, he was waving a phone receiver at her.

"You have a call." He raised one black eyebrow and handed her the phone.

A woman's softly accented voice came on. "I hope I'm not bothering you, Miss Robbins. This is Miss Makarova's companion. I am also her translator. I arrived after you have left. Natasha wants to be sure that you understood her today and apologize for not being able to continue speaking with you. She's not confident of her English yet."

"Please thank her for her time. Her English is expressive of how she feels."

"Yes, but Miss Makarova asks me to say that it is not personal dissatisfaction but artistic hopes she was talking about to you. She is thankful for all that friends and ballet world does for her. The true artist can never be satisfied, but in her life, she is happily engaged to be married. She does not want to give a wrong impression that she's not grateful for opportunities"

Then Makarova's huskier voice came over the line.

"I forget to say that Anthony Tudor is greatest friend and chorcographer. He will create ballet for me. Anthony and I, we both speak language of *nuance*." She gave the word a soft French elongation, held slowly aloft as she held an arabesque.

"I hope he will. Perhaps with Rudolf Nurcyev? A new ballet for you together?"

Geneva saw Connor lean forward and nod encouragement.

"Perhaps, we cannot say," came Makarova's reply.

"Thank you again. Perhaps we can speak another time."

Geneva's hand was shaking when she placed the phone in its cradle. "I'm star-struck. I didn't know being so close to her would have this effect."

"You did better than you credit yourself for. You need vodka and an order of caviar, maybe a bowl of borscht?"

Geneva nodded and Connor signaled the waiter.

"I didn't want to impose myself. I wanted to be a fly on the wall. She's more beautiful and frail up close than when you see her on stage."

"What did she say at the end when you asked about Rudi?"

"She didn't respond. Do you think that they'll dance together?"

"It's happening. They're dancing in London in three weeks. You'll be there."

"London?"

"Yes, in July, less than a month to pack."

"I don't take three weeks to pack." Geneva smiled.

"Lucky you. Packing consumes me. Open this before the food comes."

He placed a slim black box on the table cloth. When she opened it, a silver tube lay inside. "Press the tip, there. Just a touch is all you need," he said.

A pin-point beam of light shone from a tiny aperture of the silver object.

"It was actually designed as a surgical tool by a friend—he does women's beauty work, a delicate task. I asked if it could be adapted to write as well as illuminate the wrinkles. Look." A bright beam shot from their table into the dim room.

"That's incredible."

"Dr. Mauricio is all that and more. I'd like to introduce him to charming Auntie."

"Why? Ruth doesn't care if she has wrinkles."

"He's very rich and they'd like each other. I'm nothing if not a matchmaker…"

"Connor! You'll find yourself up against the most stubborn woman. And thank you, I can write in the dark with this." Geneva turned it over in her palm. "It's always hard to read what I scribble in the dark." She pressed down and wrote in her notebook.

"Just now, her companion told me Makarova is engaged to be married. I wonder who it is. She has such a fragile body, it's hard to imagine..."

"Being crushed in love, you mean? Do you see her like yourself?"

Geneva blushed. "Don't tease. I'm as solid as she is crushable."

She was saved from saying more by the arrival of a steaming bowl of borscht.

———

"Miss, look at me and hold very still." Najiba the hairdresser wet her finger with something dark and gently outlined Geneva's lower lid with kohl. She plucked Geneva's brows, defined them, applied mascara and put a coat of red polish on her short nails.

"I hardly recognize myself."

"Like Cinderella," answered Najiba. "You will meet your prince."

"When will I turn back into a pumpkin?"

Najiba laughed and accepted ten pounds. "Never, my pretty."

Outside, the Thames flowed with a dark pull toward the night. Bells from the city's churches began ringing seven as she entered the foyer of the Royal Opera House where she almost ran into the queue of standees who were waiting to be let in. She recognized some of the balletomanes she knew in New York—faithfuls who were in London for this historic partnership between the Russian defectors—but they didn't recognize her.

She realized she was dressed and made up so differently from her usual skirt, blouse, flat shoes and skinned-back bun, that she might as well have been in a disguise.

"I came for Margot as Juliet and discovered I was going to see Makarova," a small woman carrying a large shopping bag said. "Nearly broke my heart."

"Makarova can't hold a candle to Margot," an elderly man in the remnants of full evening dress answered. "I expect to be under-whelmed but I couldn't stay away."

"What's all the fuss?" a small man with a big voice asked. "Nureyev can't make a proper landing. With Erik Bruhn, Natasha had a real prince. Nureyev is a rubbish man."

A Nureyev fan said, "Bullocks," and Geneva thought they might come to blows when a stout lady with a flower-bedecked hat stepped between them.

"It's high time the Queen Bee moved on. Bring on the Russian fireworks."

The voice level rose, exclamations for and against their favorites. Geneva found the balletomanes' gossip, even if unreliable, was informed by experience and often more insightful than published critics. Some of these fans had traveled the world, following their favorite with the fierce attachment of a parent, for whom they would be sacrificing other comforts. They told competing stories of moments their idol acknowledged them with a smile or a word, and how they collected the slightest item the dancer might have worn. In New York, Geneva once visited an apartment where ballet slippers and ribbons, pressed flowers, programs and photographs, were set off in sanctuaries with candles and incense. Balletomanes, like art investors, held stakes in their love objects. The difference was that they only possessed their treasures in memories.

Geneva climbed stairs and found her seat in the box circle. Across the shimmery sea of lights and colors below was the curtained Queen's Box. She shivered.

At her side, she felt someone's body warmth, looked up and saw a tall thin man with a clipped beard and a hat in his hand.

"The lady is alone?"

"Albert?"

Albert Roth leaned down, brushed her ear with his lips, gave her a kiss on the part of her hair. She was shocked. How had Albert found her?

"I watched a woman come in who looked both familiar and unknown. If I hadn't been advised to buy this seat, I would have let her go as an actress, admired from afar."

"Albert! I'm totally surprised. You're growing a beard?"

"I've declared myself a Freudian, but I'm not as changed in two months as you."

Albert Roth was a resident in psychiatry at Stanford. He and Geneva had met at the Opera House in San Francisco the first time she traveled to see Natalia Makarova in *Swan Lake*. Albert was a passionate ballet goer—passionate enough to have sobbed in the seat next to her when Odette was being torn from Siegfried's arms. That night, he'd been intended to recognize his blind date at the first intermission by the red carnation she wore. Geneva had also worn a single red flower pinned on her jacket though hers wasn't meant as more than decoration, a gift from the doorman at her hotel as she left for the ballet. Once they'd begun talking at the end of the first act, Albert never left Geneva's side. He threw his flower over the railing and kissed Geneva before the end of the ballet. "I have escaped Mother's plan," he told her. They had stayed in touch with phone calls between New York and Palo Alto, so he'd known Geneva was in London but never said he might come to join her. He seemed, she thought, to love throwing himself into unplanned action.

"I had three days off on my rotation. Your aunt gave me the phone number for *Icarus* and your boss told me you'd be here, in this very seat tonight. I should probably have pretended it was all magic, like San Francisco."

Geneva thought of the two fairy godmothers dressing her up to meet a dark prince. Albert fit the description, even more so with his new beard.

"I think your boss flirted on the phone," Albert whispered.

"That's Connor, he's a flirt."

"An entertaining conversation. I look forward to meeting the genius at *Icarus*."

Albert handed Geneva a red rose, leaned over to insert it in the lapel of her suit, then placed one in his own jacket. "In honor of our first meeting. I know you were wearing a carnation but these are what I bought from a flower seller." He again kissed her ear and she remembered his smell, very clean but not doctor-like, not medicinal.

She squeezed his hand. "I have much to tell you, and I'm so glad you're here but I'll need to concentrate during the performance and probably work tonight. Connor wants me to get this in before I go to Paris."

"He didn't say anything about Paris," Albert said. Geneva thought she heard resentment in his voice. She quickly told him that she hadn't known Nureyev and Makarova would be performing again so soon. "It's been scheduled for the courtyard of the Louvre Museum in a little over a week from now. I've never been to France. I hadn't been to London, either."

The house lights blinked on and off.

Geneva squeezed his hand. He kissed her fingers, sending chills down her spine

Natalia Makarova stepped onstage in Juliet's sheer, high-waisted dress, the ungainly wig replaced by a simple, close-fitting cap with light brown curls down the back, held by a ribbon. Geneva thought she looked barely fifteen and eager to love.

What happened next totally surprised her: more than eager, Juliet showed no hesitancy, nothing of the virgin daughter kept under protective family scrutiny. Makarova rolled her eyes and ogled the young men on the stage. She made it clear she was ready for excitement. *Fébrile.* Geneva jotted the word. High strung. A flirt, a *cocotte*. When she caught sight of Romeo, she flew to him without restraint, making a risky and impetuous leap. Nureyev barely caught her. *Making him pay*, Geneva wrote quickly.

Precipice, Geneva wrote in her notepad as the first act ended with Juliet hanging off the stage balcony as if she might hurl herself from it.

Geneva wrote questions. *Nureyev? Reversal?*

"Shall we drink champagne?" Albert asked.

"Will you hold on just a minute." She held up her hand. "Let me just get this down." She wrote and when she looked up, she saw a scowl of impatience on Albert's face. Then he stood up. "I'll be waiting for you."

She found him holding two glasses of champagne in the foyer.

"Bubbly is going flat," he said.

She scribbled more but didn't touch the champagne. "Almost done. Get everything down, Connor says. Write it up fresh."

Albert scowled with his brows and chin clenched. "I know you didn't expect me but I hoped for more of a welcome." He drank down her champagne as well.

"Tomorrow we'll have the day together, and tomorrow night there's another performance. I can't wait to tell you how crazy it's been. You'll understand then."

"There isn't much time," he said. "I've one more day."

They returned to their seats and didn't speak again until the short interval between Acts Two and Three. She covered her small pages, wrote more. *Feverish. Throws Nureyev off pace. Mad as Giselle Will N answer*?

When the curtain fell on the mourning families, a subdued applause followed and

Geneva wrote, *strange quiet.*

She turned to ask Albert what he thought but the seat next to her was empty. She was glad he'd gone ahead to give her time to write before she met him in the lobby.

In the foyer, she didn't see him. Albert was tall so she

should have been able to pick him out of the crowd by his height. Maybe he'd gone down to the ground floor lobby. She also needed a moment to freshen up.

As she waited her turn in the ladies' room, she decided she had to see Makarova, to explain the inadvertent disturbance with Nureyev. Albert would understand and wait. She didn't know what she'd say to the ballerina but she had to apologize, and then to ask what had inspired—inflamed—her Juliet tonight.

She still didn't see Albert as she made her way outside to the stage door. It was cold and she rushed ahead to a light where a man stood. She showed her press credentials and was allowed back stage.

Makarova was removing mascara and shadow with one hand, holding her long cigarette holder in the other. A towel folded over her shoulders fell across her small chest. Buckets of flowers, costumes, and toe shoes filled every inch.

"Did I dance well tonight, you think?" Makarova didn't turn from the mirror.

"You were a very exciting Juliet. You gave her flair."

"Flair. That is showy?"

The dancer exhaled a long stream of smoke as she tissued makeup from her face.

"First act, I am dancing intuitively, really spontaneously, try to find myself. You know, little time for working with Rudi but we are professionals." She paused. "Sometimes a partner gives nothing, then I must do for self." She laughed. "I succeed?"

"Very different from..."

"From Margot Fonteyn. Yes, of course you can say that."

Makarova waved her hand. "Time to go. Friends come now." She gestured with her cigarette holder. "Go now."

Feeling humiliated by dismissal felt worse because she knew she deserved it. She backed out into the corridor where she pressed herself to a costume rack.

After some minutes, Makarova emerged in a clinging black dress, black boots, and boa thrown over her shoulders. She had outlined her eyes, deepened them with shadow and kohl, wrapped her hair under a gold and black turban, her profile imperious as smoke curled up from her long black cigarette holder.

This time, Geneva followed the maze of inner corridors back to the lobby where ushers were picking up programs from the floor. She searched the faces at the bar, not seeing Albert. Where had he gone? If he weren't in the theater, perhaps he was in a nearby pub waiting for her, but there were dozens of pubs in the Covent Garden district.

The paving was wet and slippery under her heels. A night fog had closed in. She thought of Covent Garden murders in a film she'd seen, how out of nowhere a man rushed up to a girl and grabbed her by the throat. They'd find her the next morning in a heap of flowers.

Geneva hurried to a waiting cab and stepped in.

Three

Since its 1841 Paris premiere, Giselle, or Les Wilis, (Théophile Gautier, librettist, Jules Perrot choreographer) has had more remarkable partnerships, more litigation and broken contracts, than any ballet in the classical repertoire. Traditionally, the male role of the noble seducer Albrecht in Giselle is secondary to Giselle. In 1910, Anna Pavlov is said to have canceled her St. Petersburg performances as the peasant girl who goes mad and dies of heartbreak because she feared being eclipsed by one particular Albrecht—Vaslav Nijinsky. After Natalia Makarova danced eleven Giselle's in a row, she vowed, "No more Giselles!" but later gave in to audience demands.

Geneva stood on the ferry deck watching dark blue water being furrowed under and surfacing in plumed white wake. All relationships seemed as ephemeral as the emerging and disappearing waves, as buffeted by doubt as the ferry's flags in the wind.

"Phone call, Miss Robbins." Geneva heard her name and took the phone.

"Hello," she shouted over static crackle, engine's rumble and waves. If it's Albert, she thought, she'd cry.

All the previous night, feeding the gas meter in her bedsit near the British Museum, she wrote and rewrote how the promise of a partnership between the Russian dancers had ended in clanging discord, while holding back her own sobs. Before dawn, she phoned Connor her tentative pages, dressed and packed to get to Victoria and catch the train for Dover.

Connor's voice sounded in a higher register against the deep thrum of the ship's engine. "Just wanted to tell you not to waver in your intentions."

"What do you mean waver, Connor? You don't want them to fail."

"Gen, dearest, from what you've written, you're only piquing my appetite for archetypal male-female combat to come. You make it clear that Rudi doesn't get his way by making nice nor Makarova by lying down. They're fighting hawks. And you, little mouse, glasses steaming, taking notes close to those divine thighs—that was High Art."

"Fighting hawks is an awful metaphor, Connor."

"Speaking of sinful earthly delights. I had a call from a fervent young man after you left New York. He hoped I'd direct him to you, which I did, down to the seat I'd reserved for you. I hope it was as rapturous as Juliet's single night."

"Albert told me you helped him. Thank you."

Connor laughed. "Albert, that's right, I'd forgotten the name. What dedication, and he reads *Icarus,* too. It appears you're enjoying drama in your life."

"I never asked for this drama. I feel like tearing my overwrought pages. They're too personal."

"The trouble started with a paranoid ballerina,

Geneva. It was your moment."

"I didn't intend to take advantage, Connor."

"You're a working girl, as they are, a professional."

"Natalia Makarova won't talk to me again. Woman to woman, I've betrayed her."

"It's not about Makarova, and it's not about you. It's chemistry, two atoms, one molecule of partnership, a vast amount of energy released in combining, or breaking up."

"I don't want to have contributed to a break up. I want them to dance together."

"Natasha survived the Soviets. She's strong as wire. She upstaged him, according to you. If you had a quickie with Rudi, it's inconsequential to her."

"A quickie! Connor, you're nasty. All I want to be is a fly on the wall watching."

"That's it, you're important *as* a fly on the wall. Don't let your feelings get in the way of a breaking story. Or use those feelings to feed it."

She snuffled and blew her nose. All she felt was exhaustion. Then she looked up.

"Oh, I think I can see France. My first time. It's so exciting. You're right, I'm getting the chance of a lifetime. Thank you."

"I wish you everything French, my dear. Auntie Ruth, by the way, is a real strumpet. She's off to Southampton with Dr. Mauricio to whom I just introduced her and they're gone to the bushes like rabbits."

"I don't believe that. Who's Dr. Mauricio?"

"The doctor of magical facelifts. The penlight. He's stealing her away from me."

"Ruth and a doctor? I don't remember him."

Connor's voice drifted off, then back. "We'll have a long chat at home. About the champagne, the ardent lover, everything."

"No bubbles left there," she said.

"You don't get rid of such an impetuous, determined fellow so easily if I know anything about men." Connor hummed the leitmotiv of *Swan Lake*—dadadadadaa dadaa dadadadadadaa—speeding up the notes so like the beginning of a horse race rather than the measured and beautiful pas de deux.

"Mademoiselle, *nous sommes ici*." The cab driver pulled to the curb. The borrowed Parisian pied-a-terre belonging to Connor's friend turned out to be a three-storied house in a neighborhood near the Palais Royal. Geneva paid and stepped out of the cab. Before she could lift her bag from the seat, a broad-faced man with dark stubble on his jowls and blue coveralls lifted it, thanked the driver, took her by the elbow and opened the gate.

Monsieur Le Brun introduced himself and ushered her into a dining room where he'd set the table, poured a bowl of coffee au lait, brought a warm baguette, a thick slab of butter, and a chunk of gooey cheese. Geneva hadn't eaten since morning in London and the first bite of warm bread, cheese and butter melted in her mouth. The caretaker opened the white-shuttered windows with bright pink geraniums hanging in pots.

"*Voulez-vous boire un verre*?" he asked, uncorking a bottle of dark red wine.

"*S'il vous plait.*"

"You speak French, Mademoiselle?"

"*Oui, un peu.*"

Geneva managed to follow Le Brun who apologized for the process of making repairs while the owners were on vacation in the south, and hoped Mademoiselle wouldn't mind the inconvenience.

"Non, non, pas de tout," she replied.

"*Août*, August," he answered. "Tout le monde goes from Paris."

Le Brun's eyes crinkled over the glass like a Gallic Walter Matthau. They sat until he returned the workman's cap to his head and picked up his tools. "Viens," he said, and she followed him down a corridor to a sunny white bedroom where a white coverlet was pulled back. She wouldn't have minded if he'd come to lie down beside her but she quickly fell asleep.

She felt a weight on her chest and sat up to breathe. The scene had been so real, from the alleyways of Covent Garden to the Esplanade where she bought her theater suit and had her hair done, that she didn't realize she was dreaming. She remembered covering miles along the river looking for Albert in a kind of hide and seek where he vanished before she caught up to him—he was looking for her as she was searching for him but taking the wrong streets, and they kept missing each other. She then saw herself lying on the pavement outside the Covent Garden box office, only instead of the flower markets, there were steps leading directly to another grey river she knew was located in Italy though she'd never been there. London, Verona and Venice were superimposed on each other like negatives of a single photograph. Romeo and Juliet, both wearing black cloaks, appeared. There were Montagues and Capulets with swords drawn standing in the background, ready to fight. She knew even as she dreamed that she was in the direct path of their fighting, the duel that would kill Tybalt and set the lovers on their path to the family crypt, but she couldn't move one way or the other. Rain pelted down and the canal began to rise. The bells of Notre Dame awakened her.

Four

The premiere of Swan Lake in Moscow in 1877 was deemed a failure: the score was too Wagnerian for Russian taste, the choreography poor, the dancing flat-footed. (The ballerina who might have saved the swan story had been sidelined for accepting jewels from a Moscow minister.) Peter Tchaikovsky died without seeing his masterpiece revived in Petersburg in 1895 with new choreography by Ivanov and Petipa: the duets and symphonic ensemble dances for Odette, the enchanted Swan Queen, her duplicitous double, the Black Swan Odile, and Siegfried, the over-mothered son who fails to see the deception, are characters who have expanded the mythic and dramatic range of ballet for the past century.

Swan Lake has undergone many choreographic transformations. A Soviet production during years of positive heroes uplifting messages might conclude with the Swan Queen and Prince Siegfried pulling off the wings of the evil magician and sailing into daylight. Nureyev (1964) and Mathew Bourne (1995) based their librettos on Prince Siegfried's dreams. After Bourne's sexually repressed Prince Siegfried makes a fateful visit to a swish nightclub where Odette in drag casts her spell, the dominatrix Odile pushes him over the edge to madness. The prince in a swirl of male swan-phantoms is finally released from life.

Monsieur Le Brun accompanied Geneva to the Metro where he went over the colored lines she should follow to reach the 18th arrondissement and the Musée Gustave Moreau. He gave her tokens and she walked into the underground, changed trains correctly and emerged at the Trinité exit at the rue de la Roche-foucauld, a tree-lined street where the white-washed brick Musée stood unobtrusively. She paid the small fee to enter the artist's jewel box of treasures, curiosities and large, gold-tinged, luminous canvasses on every inch of wall.

At first, Geneva didn't particularly like the pale female figures in historic and mythological dress crowded one beside the other. They seemed too much like sentimental illustrations for a romance novel or poster art on calendars. But as she wandered the main exhibition room and climbed the spiral staircase, Geneva continued to feel the heroines of Moreau's dramas-in-paint staring at her—a pale Sphinx as enigmatic as her name before Oedipus; Desdemona in her chamber with Emilia; Ophelia drifting downstream under flowers. The effect was disturbing, as if the viewer could also hear these abandoned and doomed women murmuring across the centuries. Moreau seemed to go deep into the psyche of heroines in their tragic selves, capturing something otherworldly, the way Natalia Makarova identified with characters who give themselves over to their fate.

As Geneva wandered through more rooms with cabinets and cases of paintings and drawings, brushes and palettes, she thought about Paris' great chronicler,

Marcel Proust, and how the courtesan Odette continually deceives poor Swann: the more love deranges him, the more he pursues the vanishing creature who changes from a daytime charmer to a night sorceress—as Odette becomes Odile the black swan. Proust had loved Diaghilev's Ballets Russes and must have known *Swan Lake*. Had anyone speculated that Odette in *Remembrances of Things Past* had been named for the Swan Queen with two natures?

She left the museum in a more tranquil mood than she'd begun the day, deciding to walk and see Paris without any particular aim. The day was sultry, sunlight diffused behind metallic clouds, not as hot as Le Brun warned it might be. On a quiet street leading from a busy crossroad, she heard heels clicking behind her. Without turning, she hurried her own steps as if fleeing from the sounds. It all came back, Albert's departure, her helplessness and failure to find him. Flood, bodies. the morning's dream. She felt her knees shaking and headed into a small park with a sign: *Saint Georges*. The heels clacking on the pavement passed the park. Saint Georges the protector. She'd be safe under his gaze until her heart stopped pounding against her chest.

Another woman approached the iron gates of the park. She was brunette, slim and well dressed. From a distance, Geneva imagined she was seeing her mother, Celia, who always wore heels, dressed in neutral colored-suits, wore a blouse with a white collar such as this woman was wearing. Celia had looked like a Parisian woman, not a hair out of place, perfectly put together. Geneva didn't know if her mother had been to Paris before the war. In another life, a life before the Nazis took over Europe, forcing her mother and Ruth into some corner of Poland that turned into Russia, Celia might have lived in a haut bourgeois neighborhood like this one, been a cultured woman, a wife, with season tickets to opera and music. She might even have performed on the piano, for which Ruth always said she had a true talent.

Ruth had saved only two pictures from her family life in Poland, photographs she'd sewn into the satin lining of the fur coat that she'd managed to keep for six years in Siberia, the coat she named her guardian bear because it had saved her from freezing. The coat came to America where Celia tried to throw it out but Ruth held on to the tattering, molting fur.

One of the pictures was a portrait of Celia's parents, Leonid and Albertine Silvernail, taken in a Warsaw studio not long after they'd married—a serious couple, both rather heavy even in youth. Albertine was a pianist and teacher at the conservatory in Warsaw. She didn't smile but there was a sweetness Geneva saw in her eyes. Grandfather Leonid, who taught mathematics in a gymnasium, looked brooding, as if he had numbers and equations on his mind. In the other photograph, two young women stood on a bridge over the Vistula River leaning against the railing. Celia and Ruth were attractive, stylish brunettes with bobbed hair that fit neatly on their heads like caps. Celia was looking away while Ruth grinned at the camera.

Geneva could never trace the geography of Celia and

Ruth's flight from the Germans on any map because, as Ruth said, borders in the east kept changing hands. "Only snow, hunger, barbed wire, soldiers we hide from," Ruth told her.

The girls were lucky: villagers who caught them in a barn didn't turn them over to the Nazis but led them to a Russian camp for refugees in Soviet territory. There a young doctor from Smolensk named Pavel Rubenstein treated Celia for frost bite. "Frozen toes, death sentence," Ruth said. "Celia and Pavel, they fell in love. I watched over older sister. Strange calm, false peace."

"When Pavel marched from refugee camp with Soviet army to fight Germans in Crimea, Celia went crazy." Ruth shook her head, remembering something she seemed unwilling to say. "I thought she dies of grief. I force her to eat my ration of bread. I make her eat."

Ruth didn't realize that her sister was pregnant. In the cold with so little food, women skipped periods. "Now it was warm. Women like trees bleed. Not Celia."

Ruth told Geneva that up to that point she herself was so small and young looking, the soldiers often mistook her for a child and let her leave the camp to forage in the woods for berries. Once, she overheard two Russian soldiers talking about the chance some of these Jews had to go abroad. Some refugees with family abroad can leave Russia to join relatives.

Ruth sent a letter to Geneva, Switzerland, where their mother Albertine had a cousin who was a violin maker. Ruth wrote his name, the city, Geneva, and "violin maker." She had no address.

"Somehow letter reaches cousin," Ruth said.

But months passed without permission from the Soviets. Celia couldn't hide the pregnancy, and lacked the strength to travel to Moscow to fill out papers for emigration. Ruth went alone. "Soviet officer said, one person in family goes." Ruth signed Celia's name, returned to the camp, gave Celia the small diamonds and money Albertine had sewn into the satin lining of the fur coat, her guardian bear.

Geneva heard the clicking of more high heels. Three older women wearing hats and gloves were speaking in rapid French, too fast for her to understand the words.

Geneva remembered how Celia recited the names for styles of footwear she sold in Lazarus Department Store in Columbus Ohio where they'd been sponsored by the Jewish Rescue Committee. *Moire* was a kind of material that looked like water. *Losenge* wasn't something you would suck for your throat but a shoe with a certain kind of heel. She thought they were the best French words before she heard arabesque and pirouette.

Celia only wished to forget what she'd endured and refused to talk about it. Until Ruth arrived, their world as Geneva remembered it, was hushed, soundless, like being locked up in airlessness. Geneva imagined her mother consigning all memories that connected her to happiness of any kind to a corner, and that corner sucked up air. Celia never said she'd been singled out for exile because she was Jewish, but before she enrolled Geneva in school in Columbus, their name had changed to Robbins. No mention was ever made of being a Jew until Ruth arrived.

"Jewish Capitalist Bourgeois Traitor," Ruth said. "They call us that. Poor Papa, he just liked his algebra."

Celia died suddenly of appendicitis before Geneva or Ruth knew she was so ill. Geneva was fifteen. At the small memorial, her mother's co-workers said she'd known more about shoes than anyone, that she was an example for them. Geneva wasn't surprised they knew nothing else about their supervisor in the fine footwear department.

In the humid August afternoon in Paris, Geneva cried for her mother who had loved beautiful things, a love she'd given her daughter without realizing it.

Geneva's thoughts circled back to Ruth, not closed off like Celia, but not forthcoming except when she chose to be. Ruth parceled out her stories like sweets.

Ruth told Geneva that after Celia got out of the camp, Soviet soldiers crammed the remaining women into cattle cars. Fall was brief, winter coming on again, and many women and children got sick from the frigid rain that dripped from the roof of the cars. When the transport reached a port on the White River, Soviet guards told them a ship was waiting to take them to an island where they'd be warm, where they'd eat bananas and oranges that grew on trees. "No, impossible," said Ruth. "I know bananas from Africa not Siberia. We are not so stupid, Sigi and I."

Sigi was a young Russian Jew who had studied German and English in Moscow.

"Sigi was smart," said Ruth. "Together we had plan." They'd been lined up to board the ship, but as soon as they saw an open door, they dashed inside where the hot and steamy air and the smell of bleach told them this was a laundry room. In darkness, they slipped washerwoman smocks over their clothes, stuffed towels to make their chests and bottoms look bigger, wrapped their heads with rags, grabbed bundles of warm wash they carried onto the deck where it began to freeze in little peaks. "Like meringue," Ruth remembered. No one stopped them from pushing past the dazed women, carrying their bundles down the gangplank where a man directed them to the village wash house in which a bent-over man with a scarred face let them in. That night, Yurik gave them bowls of soup and bread. He told them they were north of Yakutsk, in the Arctic Circle. "There were no bananas," said Ruth.

Yurik was a political exile allowed to work. He hid Ruth and Sigi in the laundry until the ship left. "We can't go anywhere," Ruth said, "No identification passports." At night, they emerged to breathe fresh air. Some nights, Yurik came to sleep with one or the other. "Sigi, me, what difference? Yurik was not bad. We were young, strong backs."

Geneva remembered feeling shocked by Ruth's lack of emotion describing what sounded like rape. Ruth brushed her hand in front of her face. "No problem," she said.

When the ground thawed, Yurik thought the girls would be safer out of town planting sugar beets in the fields. "Sigi and me, we stole sugar, traded for vodka, got more food, one time, lipstick, called Beauty, in silver tube. We were still normal girls. We liked pretty things."

Geneva always imagined her aunt as a fox-like creature who could move at night unseen. After the story of the lipstick, the fox had blood-colored lips and smiled.

At the end of the war, Sigi wanted to take Ruth with her to relatives in Israel, but by then Celia had found out where her sister was and sent a ticket to Columbus, Ohio. "America. I dream of machinery of America," Ruth said.

Twice in her life, Ruth had visited Sigi, and once her friend from exile came to New York. Sigi was matronly, with hennaed hair and tight clothing even in summer. Ruth never looked anything but uniquely stylish, whether she wore overalls or a suit and high heels to drink champagne and eat caviar in the Tea Room.

Geneva got up from her bench and began to walk. She felt relieved to have turned from the gloomy memories of Celia to thinking of Ruth, which made her smile. At a news kiosk, she bought a copy of *Saisons de la Danse,* a glossy picture magazine with Maya Plisetskaya as Swan Queen Odette on the cover. Amazing luck, Geneva thought when she read that Plisetskaya and the Bolshoi Ballet were dancing *Swan Lake* that night. This couldn't have been planned better. Two Russian Swan Queens in one week.

———————

Maya Plisetskaya made her entrance on the Odeon stage as if her enchantment in the winged bird body captured soul as well as flesh. She radiated cold and fear, until the moment the prince touched her and she began to thaw, heat suffusing her fingers, her shoulders trembling, then rising, filling out, as if like alchemy, his touch transformed a swan into a woman.

During the interval between the acts, Geneva stepped into the lobby and was walking toward the refreshment counter when she stopped and stood motionless. On one side of the hall stood Yuri Grigorovich, director of the Bolshoi Ballet, a small man with a furrowed brow, dressed in a black suit too large for his frame. Rudolf Nureyev, wearing doeskin and thigh-high taupe boots the color of creamed coffee, a garnet lamé scarf wrapped turban-like around his head, was striding in Grigorovich's direction. Alongside Nureyev, three companions'—Madame Veliani, fire red hair and lips, and an androgynous couple, tall, spectral in tuxedo and black tails, white-faced, slicked-back hair, out of *Cabaret*—strolled in unison. Nureyev's eyes, outlined in kohl, stared at his former compatriot, the Soviet choreographer. At the last minute, the quartet swerved.

Geneva kept her head down just in case Nureyev might think of putting her on notice again, but the dancer and his entourage were too engaged displaying how they disdained the Soviet bureaucratic suits. The major director of Soviet ballet and the man he must consider a traitor never looked at each other. Would they have spoken if they'd been alone? Geneva wondered.

The bell rang to return for Act III. Plisetskaya, now in Odile's black feathers, brandished her fan like a whip as she seduced the prince with such steely arrogance and absolute control that triumph over innocent love was easy. From her jeweled fingers to her long proud neck, Plisetskaya ruled. *Fearlessness,* Geneva wrote in her notebook.

The next night Geneva stepped into the great walled Cour Carrée du Louvre. An oppressive weather had arrived with humidity and heavy threatening skies. Maya Plisetskaya had performed in the relatively intimate space of the Odeon Theater, but Natalia Makarova would have the vast darkness of the open air court where crosscurrents of air already swirled papers in small gyres.

Geneva couldn't believe the choice of such a terrible location; even if the show in August was meant for tourists come for a spectacle, the Cour Carrée was too vast and unprotected for an intensely psychological ballet. Technicians mounting banks of lights around the perimeter had to brace themselves against the wind. Far up on the stone steps, the lights below would pinpoint a tiny soloist like a deer in headlights. Bad omens, bad vibes, Geneva thought. More suited to gladiatorial contests. *Deer in headlights*.

When Makarova made her entrance as Odette in Act II, she seemed to be taking her cue from the weather, shivering and fearful, a captive who foresaw her doom. Geneva watched as Nureyev gently coaxed the Swan into his arms, fear rippling from her rib cage to her trembling fingers, trembling even to the egret feathers on the sides of her small head. Afraid, amazed, she gave herself over entirely to human touch, swooning in the prince's arms, bending and swaying, nearly folding herself in two.

Her long neck and small head curved back to her spine, her body swathed in tulle floated with her arabesques, motion more than substance in the lights.

Moreau's doomed heroine, Geneva wrote.

Makarova's image of human love felt so intimate, so trancelike. With each quivering battement, it was if she were undressing her soul and her body before Nureyev. *I give myself to you, do with me what you will*, Geneva wrote without taking her eyes from the stage. Finally her enchanter, the magician Rothbart, broke the trance as he tore Odette from Siegfried's arms. The stage went black amid misty exhalation of dry ice.

During the interval, Geneva felt relief mixed with trepidation. The act had gone perfectly without any sign of dissension between the dancers. Makarova seemed to have let herself trust Nrueyev and he was accepting her.

Geneva watched a small army of blue jumpsuits dry the stage because the mists left a dangerous film on the wooden boards. Then, as everyone returned to their seats, a male voice announced that cold weather and slick stage made it too dangerous for the ballerina to perform the famous 32 fouettés, a signature sequence of bravura dancing. Dread, not relief, filled Geneva when she heard these words because she knew how contrary Nureyev could be if anyone changed the program without his approval. He was brutal to ballerinas who didn't perform as planned.

The first images of the magician's court should be dark and sinister, but the director flooded the scene with white light. All wrong, Geneva thought. Odile needed illusion, shadows and dark corners to work her seduction.

When Makarova made her entrance as Odile, her stiff black feathers and sequins glittered in the hard light but Geneva knew right away that the ballerina hadn't fully left Odette behind. She must inhabit, as Plisetskaya had done, both Odette, the vulnerable White Swan in the forest, and Odile, the Black Swan, the deceitful creature of the magician. Much more than a costume change, the ballerina had to transform flesh back into a carapace, to revert from woman to snake-bird. Makarova's Odile was more like a girl held captive in a harem, a girl made to perform a vulgar dance, a burlesque for her supper, than the seductress determined to humiliate a foolish prince. *She'll have to do better to seduce this Siegfried,* Geneva scribbled.

Even without the fouettés, Odile had to execute several difficult sequences of rapid leaps and pirouettes, all fast tempo. Geneva watched, almost without breathing, as Makarova whirled toward Nureyev who caught her in mid-turn. On a second approach, she canted forward, barely reaching his hand in time. The third gyre, Makarova whipped around two, three times. She reached for Nureyev to stop her momentum. He didn't move. He wasn't standing quite close enough to catch her without taking perhaps two steps forward. He didn't take those steps. Makarova lost her balance and began to fall.

Oh my god! Geneva stood up. Others were on their feet as Makarova seemed to fall in slow motion, to fall forever under the spotlight in a vast darkness before thousands of people. When her head hit the stage, they all heard it. The recorded music stopped, which made the human silence even louder. No one moved.

Rudolf Nureyev stood no more than a few feet from Makarova's fallen body but there he stood, making no move to help her to her feet. He didn't kneel at her side, nor extend his hand. Rather, he stood, hands on his hips, feet apart like a ballet master who has watched a student take a dive that would teach her to be more careful.

At last, Makarova began to inch her way back up from the stage, her hand at the nape of her neck, her shoulders raised, fingers testing vertebrae along her spine. She shook her ankles and feet, and without a look at Nureyev, waited for the taped music, the cymbals and thunder crashing, to recommence the Black Act. There was no connection between them now. Makarova made her steps, her turns small and careful until she reached the moment of seduction that emotionally never took place. Siegfried lifted his two fingers in the absurd vow that signaled his mistaken transfer of affection to Odile. Geneva was sure she saw irony in his expression.

The act ended in darkness and crashing symbols and they were all mercifully released from suffering.

———

Geneva spent the next day walking the 4th and 5th arrondissements, replaying the scene, everything happening over and over in slow motion, the ballerina's first off-balance pirouette, the second even more dangerously tilted turn. She stopped the mental replay on the third pirouette, the instant Makarova lost her balance, unable to bear it. A gust of wind might have moved her out of

Nureyev's reach. Or the moisture on the stage caused her toe to slip beneath her. Geneva entertained the possibilities of several unpredictable seconds, but she remained sure that Nureyev could have caught his partner.

The *Son et Lumiere* schedule called for Nureyev to dance *Swan Lake* in rotation with a triad of alternating partners—two French prima ballerinas, *étoiles* as they were called, followed by Makarova again the third night. Geneva should have stayed away, but when dusk fell, despite a cold she'd caught the night before, she headed toward the Cour Carrée. Again the night was overcast, starless, cold and damp.

Before she found her seat, Trudy Weiss, a German photographer she knew from New York, tapped on her shoulder.

"You saw the fucking bastard let her fall?"

Geneva nodded. "You did, too?"

"Men are shits. It's so goddam cold tonight. In fucking August."

"Did you get a photo by any chance?" Geneva asked.

"Here, on the ground, I have her. With the bastard standing there, you see?" Trudy pulled out her folder from her shoulder bag to show Geneva negatives. Together they held them up, and with the help of Geneva's flashlight, the both clearly saw Nureyev standing several feet away looking down at Makarova on her back. The photo in negative looked like a doctor's x-ray.

"The evidence," Trudy said.

"It is. Would you send copies to New York? *Icarus* will pay."

"Ya, ya, sure. Tomorrow. We go watch, then get a drink," Trudy said.

Geneva could barely sit through Act II with the first of the French ballerinas. Every time Nureyev jumped or turned, the crowd applauded for so long that the taped music had to be restarted. *Not my gallant Prince*, Geneva scribbled in her notebook. She was glad she'd given Trudy the address to send the photographs because the German was leaving Paris the next day and Geneva got away before the intermission ended.

———

The night Makarova performed again, Geneva saw the ballerina was dancing in pain, barely able to complete her arabesques in the White Act. A voice on the loud speaker again announced that she would omit the fouettés in the Black Act. A group near the stage booed, a group Geneva felt sure was Nureyev's awful clique. On the stage, the principal dancers looked past each other, as chilly as the night air.

———

The following day, the Ballet Opéra management threatened to fine Makarova for cutting short the Black Act. Nureyev told a *Le Monde* reporter, "I dance every night, bad back or good. Dancer owes it to audience to push and dance through injury."

Makarova answered with a press release. "I'll never

dance with that man again, never. I am used to ballet that
is refined and a partnership must be refined, flexible, sen-
sitive. Perhaps it is difficult for a man who is thirty-five."

She added that her doctor had ordered rest. She flew
off to New York.

Nureyev hurled the final insult in print. "It does less
harm to let ballerina fall on her derriere than for woman
to land badly in partner's arms and injure his back."

The *Herald Tribune* seemed to revel in what they
called "The Battle of the Ballet Stars." Madame Veliani
was quoted, "Rudolf Nureyev had to follow the ballerina's slow tempo. Enough was enough. I shall remove
the Makarova picture from my wall."

In another front page photo, Geneva thought the
scar on Nureyev's lip looked like a curling vicious worm.

Suddenly the weather warmed, became humid, then very
hot, more typical of August. Geneva had a full-blown
cold and wrote with boxes of tissue at her side. She typed
as fast as her fingers could hit the keys to get the story to
Connor by the time Trudy's photo arrived. Monsieur Le
Brun made coffee, brought her croissants, worried she
wasn't eating. She thanked him and kept working. When
she finished, Le Brun took her packet to be mailed by a
special post. She felt a great relief seeing it go. Connor
would share her outrage. They would skewer Nureyev
for his boorishness, his betrayal.

Part Two

Five

Mikhail Fokine created the The Dying Swan for Anna Pavlova in St. Petersburg in 1905. The Swan's life and death in four minutes of fluttering arms and bourrée suivi—little steps following each other—became Anna Pavlova's signature ballet, which she performed at least 4000 times, from the world's greatest stages to rural outdoor movie theaters transformed by car headlights. Pavlova's technical mastery mattered, the choreographer Fokine said, but the reason the work transfixed audiences was the emotion, the struggle of "the soul to live." On her death bed, Pavlova is reported to have whispered, "Prepare my swan costume."

Connor opened the conversation complaining about the New York heat wave. "I'm leaving for Fire Island tomorrow and after that, thinking of flying over to take you to Venice for Peggy Guggenheim's show. Maybe we'll follow Marcel and Odette through the city. Your image of the swan connection might be original."

"What about the images of Makarova flat on her back?"

"Gruesome. How's the weather?"

"Unpredictable. So cold when Nureyev dropped Makarova that my breath felt solid in the air. Then it turned steamy, like New York." She coughed. "So you got Trudy Weiss' pictures."

"As I said, gruesome. Anything wrong, Geneva?"

"You said gruesome? You've read my story?"

"Oh yes, right here on the table with a sheaf of clippings from Paris. Silent ballet dancers can be quite a noisy bunch."

"I hate the public controversy but I'm glad she was willing to speak out and defend herself. Of course, it doesn't change what happened."

"And exactly what did happen, my dear?"

Geneva was silent. He had the pictures. Why did he ask? "Nureyev dropped her."

"Gen, let me speak and don't interrupt. In print, we are calling it an unfortunate accident, and we won't say *drop* but *missed cue*, or we risk being sued for libel."

"Will you repeat that? I'm not sure I understood. What *accident*?" She coughed.

"You are ill. You know I can't stand it when people around me are sick."

"I'm thousands of miles away, Connor, and I'm choking on your words. I'm telling you something that I saw happen and that I wrote accurately for *Icarus*."

"Your writing, excellent as always. A few edits and it goes to print."

"A few edits? What edits?"

"The wording will be, 'An unfortunate accident.' A few cuts here and there."

"No, I'm telling you, Connor, he let her fall. I talked to several Opéra dancers who saw everything from the stage. The corps dancer closest to the scene said Nureyev made no move to stop Makarova from falling. I sent quotes, their words."

"I'm aware of the vividness of your imagination which usually I herald."

"Imagination! I didn't make up anything. He let her drop like a stone and then stood there watching her."

"Geneva, darling, there is a world of difference between accident and intent."

"There are witnesses. You weren't there. I was. Why are we arguing?"

"I believe I said liability. Even with witnesses, an intentionally malicious act is one thing, an accident, even a preventable accident—though I don't say this was preventable—another. We're the printed word, not ballet gossip."

"Ballet gossip! You love gossip more than truth." She coughed, sputtered, resisted blowing her nose in the phone but wishing she were close enough to infect him. "You call sticking a knife in someone accidental?"

"You are losing all perspective and confabulating metaphorical weapons. Beyond libel, your story will be unpopular with our readers."

"Do they want pandering? Connor, if you could have seen Nureyev standing hands on his hips like Napoleon, you'd have no doubts."

"I like Napoleon. Listen, Geneva, Makarova is famous for making her partners adjust to her tempo. That might work with Ivan Nagy or Bruhn but Rudi didn't go along, or only for so many performances, as you so richly described his patience in London."

"Paris was different from London."

"Because Nureyev was trying to make the best of a difficult situation, a woman who upstaged him. In Paris, she misses a beat, gets behind time, the stage is wet, she slips and takes a tumble. The bruises on her bony little tushie must be better because she's rehearsing with Nagy in a mid-town studio for the fall ABT season. Aren't you relieved, Gen, that she wasn't injured and that all can be forgotten?"

"Never forgotten!" Geneva shouted. "She's being tough. Injuries linger. He was guilty of breaching a sacred trust between artists."

"I know that *Swan Lake* is a morality play for you, now extended to Natasha's honor—womankind's honor—but you're conflating a mistake on stage with men wronging women and this I won't publish without edits, with or without your permission."

"Men like you and Nureyev betray women."

"Ah, so this is the question again. We don't seem to bury it."

"It's not about me. You're abetting, excusing, artistic assassination."

"Enough character assassination. I'm trying to talk sense to a professional writer, not resolve the age-old man versus woman story." Connor cleared his throat "*Icarus* won't print accusations."

"You're betraying me." She tried to keep her voice steady as her lips quivered.

"I'm sorry but I'm going to end this conversation.

The jitney will be here any minute. How I love the island the last weeks of August, knowing we're heading into a season, lots of dance coming in September, new hem lengths on the avenues."

"Truth isn't a hem length that goes out of season."

"Is this a difficult time of the month, my dear?"

"That is you at your most misogynistic!" Geneva said so loudly Le Brun looked up. "She was wronged. Nureyev is a menace. He's responsible for a ballerina's injury."

What Geneva heard next sounded like static over the line. The noise continued until she realized she was hearing Connor tearing up her pages. With each tear, she imagined Makarova's white tutu, white strips of stiff fabric, being ripped to shreds.

"You just destroyed my work!"

"I'm your editor and publisher. It's lonely on the golden throne."

The line went dead. She stared out at the garden that hummed with bees in the honeysuckle. She hadn't told Connor that she had a carbon copy. No more *Icarus* in her life. She'd live with that as long as someone published the real story.

"Madame is not ill? The bad news?" Le Brun unfastened his tool belt and took the phone from her hand. "*Ca va, ma petite,*" he said, stroking her head. His bulkiness, his baggy brown eyes and wine breath felt so reassuring she let herself go limp in his arms.

Six

La Bayadère or The Temple Dancer premiered in St. Petersburg in 1877 (choreography Marius Petipa, score Ludwig Minkus). The ersatz Hindu melodrama, a Giselle with bangles, was a hit for its opulence and classical "white" second act, an opium-laced dream of reunion in the afterlife called "Kingdom of the Shades." The ballet fell out of favor until 1980 when Natalia Makarova restaged the dream-sequence for ABT; not to be outdone, Rudolf Nureyev produced the entire ballet in 1992 in Paris, only three months before he died.

What were the chances that another tired female passenger on the shuttle from La Guardia would have *Icarus* open before her? Some tiny fraction of one percent must know the rarified arts magazine existed or afford to buy it, Geneva thought, but there sat a middle-aged woman holding an umbrella in one hand, rubbing her eyes with the other, her short legs firmly planted on the bus floor in worn solid shoes, *Icarus* open before her. All Geneva could see was the cover, Natalia Makarova, chin in hand, eyes luminous and dreamy, and it gave her a sense of validation—that she was a writer valued enough to have the featured story.

Wait until you get to where Nureyev drops Makarova, Geneva wanted to say to the woman she imagined was a Russian, with a past as a dancer, or maybe a teacher. Then she remembered that no one would be reading about the betrayal in Paris because it wasn't being printed in *Icarus*. This was the previous issue, Connor's assemblage of interviews with Makarova from the Mayflower Hotel and her minutes in the Queen's box with Nureyev. She couldn't bear to think of the sycophantic voice that was her own. The thrill of being read that lifted her high now felt flat, like champagne losing its fizz and turning into a headache that lasted all the way into Manhattan. A deeper, duller hurt came over her: she probably wouldn't see her byline in *Icarus* again.

On the dining table of their apartment lay a note from Ruth saying that she'd gone to the shore for the weekend and would be back later in the day. How could Ruth not welcome her home after more than three weeks in Europe? Was she off in the sun with Connor? Geneva couldn't stand the thought that her closest relative and the only person who loved her completely was colluding with her enemy. Or maybe she was reading too much into her aunt's absence. Ruth loved the water and swam fearlessly but now Geneva imagined her dark head bobbing in the waves as breakers submerged her until all there was to see was an unsteady horizon.

Geneva lay listening to the air conditioner chugging

cool air into the apartment, wanting to fall asleep but too tired and upset to let herself go. Each time she seemed to be falling into unconsciousness, she brought herself back with a start. But she must have slept because when she opened her eyes, the light barely came in their east-facing windows. She hadn't re-set her watch to New York time but guessed five o'clock.

A buzzer sounded from the lobby.

"Special delivery box downstairs for you," the door-man, Norton, said over the intercom.

Geneva checked to make sure her two suitcases were where she'd left them by the door. "Maybe it's meant for 4-F."

"Miss Geneva, got your name on it. Says from Mr. Connor."

"I'll be down later to pick it up . I'm tired right now. Thanks, Norton."

The doorbell rang a few minutes later. Norton held a box about three feet high and as wide.

"Norton, that's too heavy."

"No, it weighs nothing."

"Thanks." Geneva took the carton. "You're right. It's light."

It occurred to Geneva that Connor was sending back all her articles but even the paper she'd written on would weigh more than this box.

"Is that all?" Norton asked.

"Yes, thanks."

Geneva rummaged around and found $5 in her bag.

"Thank you, Miss," he said. "Welcome home."

Inside the box, Geneva discovered Connor's balsam-wood stage set of *Swan Lake* nestled in cotton and tissue. She unwrapped five tiny figurines, swanlets in white tutus with thread-thin feathers attached to the backs of their miniature heads. The Swan Princess herself was white from head to ballet slippers, egret feathers around her coiffure, perfect in every detail.

Geneva's hands trembled as she placed the swanlets around Odette to await the prince. The set included snow-crusted trees, also beautifully carved from balsam wood, everything as delicately fashioned as a ship in a bottle.

In the box, she saw Connor's handwritten note. "*Kiss and make up.*"

Geneva went to the stereo and placed her LP of Eugene Ormandy with the Philadelphia Orchestra on the turnstile. Carefully, she moved the needle to the second band, the opening of Act II, Siegfried's entry into the forest. She lifted out the prince in his black tunic and white legs and stood him in the middle of the set. A virgin prince, she thought, torn between his mother's rules and nighttime fantasies, makes his escape from maternal supervision into the forest where he loses his cosseted self to passion and danger. Were all men Siegfrieds, running away from Mother, flinging themselves at the first image of love, besotted as any in *Midsummer Night's Dream*? As the oboe mourned and heavier strings prefigured the futility of breaking the magician's enchantment, visions of Makarova on the cold dark stage again filled Geneva's head. Wild swans, overarching flights, arabesques, a crash.

The deceptive waltz that began Act III was so full of

sharp and harsh notes that any dancer, any viewer, would continue at their own risk. Geneva pulled the needle off the LP. She couldn't endure the tension.

A moment later, the door opened and Ruth walked in carrying a grocery bag that she put down to hug Geneva. She had a new short haircut and wore a polka dot red and white halter top and white shorts. She smelled of sun and sea, with the freshness of basil she carried in her hands.

"We stopped at farmers' stand for tomatoes. You hungry?"

"I was worried you might have drowned. Were you with Connor?"

"Not me," Ruth answered, "I don't see Connor. What is this you have?" Ruth came to look down at the stage set.

"It's a real treasure but I don't understand why Connor sent it since he fired me, or I quit, or both, which I'm sure you've heard all about."

"No, Connor says nothing. Let's eat now."

———————

"This is delicious, thank you. I was starved." Geneva bit into crusty bread and sweet earthy tomatoes and bright basil drizzled with olive oil. Ruth added pillows of fresh mozzarella to her chunk of bread.

Ruth lit a cigarette and got up to gather the plates. "Dr. Mauricio comes to New York from time to time. I go with him to Hamptons."

"Isn't he married?" Geneva asked. Ruth nodded.

"Why is it that not one of us, Celia or you or me...

why don't we get married?"

"Celia didn't trust loving another man. I don't need husband. You? Who knows?

You are not like Celia. Not like me."

"Ruth, what kind of doctor was my father?"

Ruth sat with her cigarette and pushed their plates aside. "In war, doctors do everything. He saved Celia's feet from frostbite."

"I know that, but what else? Was he tall or short?"

"Darling, it is long ago to remember. No cameras, no pictures from that time. Pavel Rabinovich liked music very much. He and Celia hummed music, quietly of course. He was not too tall. Good looking, Yes, handsome man, too young for dying."

"You know for certain that my father is dead?"

"Jewish doctor from Moscow who went with Red Army to Crimea? What are chances? Even if Pavel by miracle survived Crimea, to survive Stalin? Double miracle."

"Pavel Rabinovich. Just to hear his name gives me chills."

"Celia changes name."

"I know, she didn't want everyone to know she was foreign and a Jew. I used to mind that but it doesn't matter now. What I think about is having a father who might be alive. Is there nothing I can do to find him?"

Ruth stared out the window.

"Ruth, the young doctor I met in San Francisco, Albert... he and I probably aren't going to see each other again."

"I speak with Albert. I like him."

"Albert came to London."

"London? He must want you." Ruth inhaled deeply.

"He cares for you."

"I don't know. I didn't pay enough attention to him and then he left without telling me. It was my fault but he shouldn't have just left."

The phone rang. Geneva jumped up. Maybe Albert.

"Geneva? Have you been playing with your doll house?"

"Connor, how could you have let this treasure leave your hands?"

"I'm not allowed to please you? Can you meet me at the Tea Room. Say seven?"

"I'm exhausted and Ruth just came home. I need to sleep."

"Don't sleep until it's dark or you'll be jet lagged for a week. I'll be the tanned handsome man in a white jacket. This won't wait."

———————

"Your eyes droop. Very Jeannie Moreau," Connor said when she sat down.

"I'm tired. I'm also suffering from disillusionment, like a French actress."

"*Non contre moi*?" He fanned his menu and fluttered his eyelashes. "Come, dear, no looking back, no Orpheus moment. The way lies ahead. I apologize for my part."

"That's easy for you. You tore the pages. I don't think apologies make up for sabotaging me and what I care about more than anything. You denied the truth."

"In the trade, the editor gets the last word. And I add, publishers get the very last word."

"I absolutely don't agree and I can't believe you're

not sorry or upset that Nureyev let Makarova fall and hurt herself?"

"She's back dancing, in the pink. We live among sharks, Geneva. I'm speaking about the life span of a story as well as the demi-gods on stage. A week after a boat sinks with everyone on board, it's forgotten."

"Nureyev is an awful man."

"At the risk of flippancy, I say let's drop it."

"Oh Connor!" Geneva put down her glass to stare at him. "How can you?"

"Write what you write so well—the human passions. Let us hear the bodices being ripped in your sentences. Keep us breathless. Make-believe, not dull middle-class morality. Ballet—constant fucking with each other and constant absolution."

"That's quite a list but you don't understand, so I suppose you won't mind if I pitch the unexpurgated Makarova story to an editor at *Viva*." She had not proposed anything to anyone but could see a sensational *Viva* cover with Trudy's picture of Makarova lying on the stage, Nureyev behind her, hands on hips.

"I own the piece and though I rejected it and will pay you a kill fee, you have no rights. Moreover, I have lawyers to make sure your story never sees print."

Geneva stood up to leave but Connor held her arm.

"I'm just warning you. The photos belong to us. You can't use them. I paid all your expenses. *Viva* is so trashy. I never said Makarova's trial by fire wasn't worth two handkerchiefs."

"You're threatening me. I'm looking forward to

freedom from bullying."

"Write a novel if you want freedom of imagination. Now drink up, this dear young man is waiting for our order."

Geneva swallowed the last of her vodka. "Trudy has negatives. The publicity alone will make the story."

She picked up her purse and walked toward the door. For one moment, she wished she had a cigarette in a very long holder to slowly light before she walked out.

Part Three

Seven

Shéhérazade, a one-act ballet to Rimsky-Korsakov's symphonic poem, was the brightest jewel in a brilliant crown that Serge Diaghilev presented for the 1910 Ballets Russes Paris season. Fokine's voluptuous choreography for Nijinsky as the Golden Slave challenged notions of masculine/feminine, human/animal, while the harem-influenced décor and exotic dress became the rage. "I never saw anything so beautiful," Marcel Proust said to a friend.

Only a short time had passed since coming back from Europe, but Geneva had never experienced such a writer's block. All she came up with, her experiences in London leading up to the night in Paris, seemed leaden, re-told, a narrative without a beating heart. It was as if her *ballon,* that impossible stay-in-the-air moment when a dancer seemed to defy gravity, deserted her.

There were still humid days left in August but cool fall weather was coming; school children would be going back to classrooms, calling out under Geneva's window. Another season in the theater and ballet would be coming up. Taking a break from writing and rewriting pages, Geneva walked down Broadway past Fairway Foods where the sidewalk display of fruits and vegetables reminded her of Paris.

She watched an old woman, already dressed for winter in a coat that reached the pavement, push a combination grocery cart and walker toward the open bins of fruit. She picked up a mango, shook her head and lifted a cantaloupe to her nose. She didn't seem to like that either, and when a clerk said, "You can't touch the fruit, ma'am," she replied that this wasn't fruit but plastic. "Melons are not in season. Do you think I'm stupid?"

Geneva smiled. The woman probably didn't have the money for Fairway and might be waiting to slip something into her basket when the clerk looked away. She knew the feeling of insecurity, how vulnerable older people were in New York. She wanted to buy something Ruth would enjoy for supper but they were economizing. Without two incomes, living on Ruth's salary while Geneva struggled to write the piece that might make money but refused to lift off and go beyond her first paragraph, scared her enough to quit moping. Today she was going to inquire about part time work at the Dance Library at Lincoln Center, but before that, there was a matinee performance of *Swan Lake* she was going to see. No casts had been announced but Geneva didn't care. It was a matter of getting herself back in shape, leaving behind the Paris disaster.

She could see herself wandering the city wearing the same moth-eaten fur coat Ruth had carried from Siberia and refused to remove from the hall closet.

"It was your grandmother's," Ruth said when Geneva, like her mother before her, wanted to get rid of the tattered guardian bear that seemed cornered in the closet like an old animal. On the subject of being old and of little use, Ruth said, either in reference to the coat or herself, "Everyone has much right to life as others. Don't become helpless." Ruth wouldn't ever be helpless—she'd tell that Fairway clerk where he could get off.

Geneva leaned against a shop window to make way for a flock of teenage girls careening down the sidewalk, wearing thigh-high black boots with stiletto heels that made them look all legs in their black hip-hugging leather pants. Two girls with purple-painted lips spewed obscenities. They made Geneva think of Persephones, unconscious of their destinies. Before long, they descended into the 72nd Street subway station, followed by a pack of boys in black.

Down Broadway toward Columbus Circle came another procession in black, some of their faces painted white like Halloween skeleton skulls. They were clanking pots and pans and other noisemakers. Through the jarring noise, Geneva heard chants. *Stop the war. Bring home our troops. Impeach Nixon.* A woman pulled a little wagon with two peach-skinned, red-haired children inside. *Stop killing babies* said the sign on the back.

Ruth read the *Times* every morning before work and the *Village Voice* on weekends. She'd marched the summer before in a demonstration against the Vietnam War—probably while Geneva was at the theater, thinking ballet was the most important thing in the world.

A man seated on a bench in the island in the middle of Broadway crooked a finger. "Girlie, come here. I have a message for you, sweetheart." Geneva hurried by.

At Lincoln Center, in the shadow of the State Theater and around the fountain, an older crowd waited for doors to open. When Geneva approached the box office, the woman inside said that *Swan Lake* was almost sold out. "It's been kept secret. Natalia Makarova is dancing the matinee. You're in luck. One seat. Third balcony."

Geneva took her ticket and entered the foyer. Inside, she climbed the stairs to avoid the elevator where she might run into someone who knew her and ask, *What did it really feel like so up close to Rudolf Nureyev? What happened in Paris?* Geneva didn't want to relive even one of those dark minutes, her crusade for Makarova, her jeremiad against Nureyev. The two Russians were dancing, Nureyev in Europe and beyond, and now Makarova in New York. If they'd put the debacle behind them, shouldn't she?

The third balcony was too far from the stage to see the expressions on the dancers' faces. She wasn't used to the ordinary seat. *Icarus* had spoiled her. Even the dimensions of the seat beneath her seemed smaller.

When the curtain rose for the court scene, the dancers and extras far below looked like puppets. Geneva didn't bring opera glasses because zooming in to one part of the stage, one dancer, made her lose the whole pattern. When Makarova fluttered onstage in Act II, her arms and head outlined in light as pure and blue as ice, there was a stillness around the ballerina that distance from the stage made even greater. Then, from somewhere below in the orchestra section, a ruckus began. Boos and catcalls. Geneva wondered if the Nureyev contingent had traveled to New York to haunt Makarova. She leaned out as far as she could to see to the ground-floor seats but felt light-headed, almost dizzy, and pulled herself back.

On the stage, Makarova appeared unruffled by the disruption. She waited a moment before she began to draw her arabesques as if her arms and legs were a delicate stylus. Ivan Nagy dancing Prince Siegfried followed her lead, courtly, never failing to be wherever she completed her phrase. The anti-Nureyev, Geneva thought.

After intermission, Natalia Makarova returned in black and sequins; although she showed none of the hesitation that had affected her Odile in Paris, she didn't capture the prince so majestically as Maya Plisetskaya had done.

Memories of the slow motion fall, of the dead-still moment when Makarova's head cracked on the stage, came to Geneva in waves. The vertigo she'd had leaning over the edge returned. She came to the theater hoping for inspiration to begin writing but she could hardly keep her eyes focused. Makarova's legs whipped around in 32 fouettés as if she'd never faltered on a wet and dangerous Paris stage, never been left by Nureyev to pull herself up from blackness.

As soon as the curtain fell, Geneva got up, holding onto the seat to keep from feeling vertigo. She left the theater after the Third Act, feeling queasy as she descended the stairs, but relieved that the beauty and style of Makarova's dancing wasn't diminished by injury.

The air was much colder as she walked across the plaza to the Library of Performing Arts. She pushed the revolving door of the library. No sign of closing, the desks and cubicles were full.

"So many people," Geneva said when Justine, a former Graham dancer who still wound her black-dyed hair in a bun and held it in place with chopsticks à la Martha, took her glasses from her nose.

"Yes, we're getting more attention. How are you? We've missed you."

Geneva felt a rush of affection. The library had been a second home she'd been in the habit of visiting two or three times a week to consult material, borrow books, or look at films. The research librarians were always ready to help.

"I should have come sooner. I guess I was too absorbed in other things."

"We've been waiting for the definitive account of the *Dark Night*," said Justine. "We heard about the skirmishes between Natasha and Rudi but it wasn't explained."

"Did that cad really drop her?" Geneva recognized the voice of Francis, an elderly Denishawn dancer in charge of archiving his company's material. Justine used to joke that Francis would go to sleep one day in the stacks and they'd find him, peaceful expression on his face, gone to dancers' heaven with his feet in fifth position.

"Is the story in the next issue?" Justine asked. "Was it too late for fall?"

"It's more complicated," Geneva said. She didn't mind so much talking about Paris in the sanctuary of the library.

"You look pale, honey," said Francis.

The librarians led Geneva to the staff room.

"Sit and tell us everything," Francis said.

"I can tell you that he did let her fall," said Geneva

"The cad," said Francis.

"He made no effort to stop her from falling. That's a fact. But you won't read that in *Icarus* because I got fired for trying to write the truth and identify the culprit."

"Not by Connor St. John! Don't tell us that." Justine sat beside Geneva.

"Connor wants to avoid libel. What happened is in the eyes of the beholder, he says, but there were witnesses up close, dancers who said Nureyev let her fall."

"What about London? That must have been fun, Geneva," said Toby, a genial man who was in charge of videos.

"I wasn't proud of myself."

"Why not? Your interview was a coup. It breathed excitement." Toby shivered.

"It distracted Makarova. I didn't realize it would, but it did."

"Natasha does follow her own tempo," said Francis.

"She was pushed to the limit and she fought back," Geneva said. "Nureyev never lifted a finger to help her when he let her fall."

Toby groaned. Francis inhaled.

"Why haven't you published it elsewhere and screw

Icarus?" asked Francis.

"I just haven't been able to. Writer's block, I guess. I can't get started."

"You were always able to find the right words, so that's serious," Justine said.

"It's no one's fault but mine." Geneva didn't know she was going to feel so helpless. Justine took her shoulders and hugged her.

"It's OK, let it out," Justine said, and Toby added, "You're among friends."

"Thank you, I know I am. It feels better to talk. I've felt gagged."

"You had a shock, my dear," consoled Toby, handing Geneva a hanky. "Maybe you've never been depressed before. We don't know our weaknesses until we're tested, but we always end up wiser, don't we? Just like broken bones heal stronger."

"That's not an image Geneva wants to hear. No broken bones," said Justine.

"I don't know what strength I have," Geneva said. "It seemed too good to be true—*Icarus*, being so close to Connor, given so much so quickly. He spent money and time training me. He edited and taught me as if I meant a lot to him and his work."

"Cinderella," said Toby. "It did happen, you have the right-sized foot."

They all laughed.

"I've got big wide feet." Geneva couldn't help showing her clogs.

"Every artist gets stuck now and then," said Justine

"I'm an artist? I've been feeling so small, my bubble punctured."

"You have to believe in yourself and your way with words," said Toby.

"You just need to regain your confidence and get back out there. I remember times when Martha nearly had to strip us bare to teach us," Justine said. "We'll help. Just let us know how we can."

"I want to apply for work here if you have it. I know I could assist other writers the way you assisted me."

"Of course, we'd love to have you, if it's what you want," said Justine.

As she was gathering up her cloak and purse to leave, Justine pulled several books from her desk and handed them to Geneva. Geneva protested that the books were new and hadn't even been shelved yet. She held up a biography with Nijinsky in his Golden Slave costume on the cover.

"We won't be needing them until Monday," said Justine. "Take care, these may be heavy. Let me give you one of our bags to carry everything in."

"They'll be back soon, I promise."

"We'll ask the director about work," said Toby.

"Thank you all very much. You gave me what I needed most." Geneva put on her cape and lifted the bag with the heavy books over her shoulder.

On the corner of Broadway and 75th, Geneva took the heavy bag from her shoulder and stepped back from traffic to wait for the light to change. She was standing in front of La Casa Alégria, a Cuban restaurant that Geneva and Ruth often visited or called for take-out. She turned to study the menu posted on the restaurant window. The day special was Ruth's favorite, curry prawns simmered in coconut milk, fried plantains, and sweetened yogurt. Geneva loved Moise's *pollo y arroz,* less spicy than the prawns. At Casa Alégria, Moise Benmayor and his wife Esther made guests feel they'd been dropped into a bi-continental café, from South Indian to Cuba, with a Jewish twist.

Geneva decided to celebrate freedom from writing, and possibly a job, by ordering both prawns and *pollo y arroz* for their supper. She was leaning down to get the library book bag and didn't see them, the three men, caps pulled down over their eyes, who ran across Broadway against the light and were upon her. They yanked at one arm for her purse, the other for her bag. She held on, even when they pushed her to the ground. As she fell, she covered her head with the cape and shoved her purse beneath her.

She felt her ribs being kicked and curse words coming from her assailants. The attackers yanked harder at her purse straps. She held on as pain ripped into her shoulder.

"Get off, you thieves!" Geneva heard the woman's voice and felt vibrations of running feet on the pavement.

Geneva looked up to see Esther Benmayor's brown arm holding a frying pan above her like a dark moon at mid-day. Esther's son Bennie, and her husband Moise, apron around his full middle and a cleaver in his hand, yelled, "*Ladrones, ladrones.*"

"Cowards," said Esther as they all watched the

attackers fleeing across traffic.

"We will tell the police they were not Cubans," said Moise.

Esther knelt beside Geneva while Moise helped her to sit up. They sent Bennie inside to call the police.

A cyclist veered to avoid them on the sidewalk. Geneva saw him look back, then ride on, head down. Across Broadway, she observed the squat, Romanesque-style First Baptist Church as if for the first time. She read the title of the sermon for Sunday, "Suffer the Little Children to Come Unto Me" as if it were written on a movie marquee.

Geneva felt certain she could get up, but her legs buckled.

"Careful," Esther said. "Stay, please. Moise, take her arm, here."

Slowly Moise helped Geneva stand. "Señorita, I think you are intact. Thanks be."

Together, the Benmayors led Geneva inside their restaurant and seated her as if she were coming for supper. She smelled freshly squeezed limes and spices of curry.

Esther Benmayor soothed Geneva with her musical Indian English as she gently washed and disinfected cuts on her arms. "I did my pre-medical training in Kerala. It's good you had on this quality wrap. It kept you from worse injury."

"I thought I might be cold coming home," Geneva answered.

"You made a wise decision. Now just stay quiet and I'll bring chai and something to eat because you need sweetness to counteract the shock."

The clock read 6:30 p.m. Only a half hour or so had passed since she left the library. Esther lit little candles, luminarias in transparent pods, on the tables, including the one where she sat.

"They didn't get my purse or my books. I was going in to order food," Geneva told the two officers when they arrived. "The men were young, they spoke Spanish."

"One had a tattoo on his right arm. I think it was a bleeding heart, something bleeding," Esther reported.

"They were not Cubans," Moise insisted. "Puerto Ricans or Dominicans—they must be. Cubans would never attack a lady three against one."

"Should have given the bag up, ma'am," said one officer who was freckled and looked very young. "They kill for less. Life doesn't mean anything to them."

The second young policemen stood to the side. "Can you move, ma'am?"

"Thanks to my friends here, I'll be fine," Geneva said. "I have my things."

"Good for you, but sometimes it's better to let go."

"No, I couldn't. The books belong to the library. I shouldn't have taken them. Not that I stole them, I'd never do that. My friends at the library entrusted them to me for the weekend. Otherwise they wouldn't have been checked out, so you see I can't lose them."

Geneva was aware she was babbling, telling the officers more than they wanted to know but she couldn't stop.

"I'm sure they'll understand, ma'am. Do you want to try moving a little or should we call an ambulance?"

"I must return the books before the library closes. Ooh," she groaned. A sharp pain from her shoulder down her left side made her wince.

"Not a good idea. You're in shock, ma'am," said one of the men. "Where do you live? We'll escort you home."

Geneva told the police her address but asked to be driven to the library at Lincoln Center. They looked at each other and then at the Benmayors. Geneva imagined them making little circles beside their heads meaning the lady is crazy.

"We'll take you where you want to go but you promise to see your doctor."

"Of course I will." *Albert,* she thought. "I have a doctor."

———

Justine and Toby were still there shelving books an hour after closing. The librarians and researchers unlocked the side door to let Geneva inside.

Geneva handed Justine the books. "Nothing got taken or damaged. They're all here. Would you tell these very nice officers that I'm all right to be left here with you? I'll get home on my own. I don't want to worry Ruth."

"You think she's OK?" The officer tapped the brim of his cap.

"She'll be fine," Justine answered. "We'll get her home safely."

"First give her brandy," said Toby. "I never should have talked about broken bones. I feel terrible."

"It's not your fault, Toby. She'll be better after the brandy, three spoons of sugar and hot water. Geneva, come and sit down. You'll take two Tylenol with it."

"Coming right up, balm and circumstance," said Toby, twirling from the room.

Justine opened a cabinet and brought out white mugs and squat brandy bottle.

The mug shook in Geneva's hand. Justine urged her to take a sip.

"Delicious, thank you." The hot, sweet drink hit her with a pleasant jolt.

Toby remained standing, waiting for more orders.

"After you left, we started talking about you. Of course we'll back you for a job but then we thought of a project you might want to take on. We'll fill you in if you're OK to listen," Justine said. "You know how highly we think of your work."

"I appreciate that." Geneva moved to get more comfortable and jumped with pain. She was beginning to hurt everywhere, yet she felt strangely clear-headed.

"You see, parents and grandparents come in all the time and ask for good books for children who are studying ballet and going to see performances. The adults want to read about the ballets with the children, especially *Swan Lake, Nutcracker* and *Sleeping Beauty*. The books must be able to stand on their own for a grown-up to enjoy and also make sense for children. The few we have are old fashioned, badly written and condescending." Justine re-filled the cup Geneva had drunk to the bottom.

"They want to relive ballet with their children," said

Justine. "Publishers ask us about finding writers but we've had no one we can truly recommend."

"In your writing, you capture what we first loved when we were children and ballet was magical," said Toby.

"I still see ballet as magical, sometimes not the dancers so much," Geneva said.

"We have all the illustrations you'd need, and there are artists looking for work if you want original material," Justine said. "Think of all the little girls who will be reading your books."

"And boys," added Toby, making a small bow.

"If you write a short proposal telling your reader about three classic ballets, I know the editor to send it to. You won't go in cold. We're behind you," said Justine.

"Russian folk illustrations," said Toby. "Can't you just see *The Firebird*? At Doubleday, Mrs. Kennedy has a hand in the production and she adores ballet."

"I saw Sadler's Wells *Firebird* when I was child in Columbus, Ohio. It was my first ballet. Also *The Dying Swan*," said. Geneva.

"They love the dance at Random House."

"There's no ill wind that doesn't blow in some good," said Toby.

"Well put," said Justine. "And now Toby, go get your nice car from the garage and drive Geneva home. Dear, I assume you have more aspirin at home. And more brandy." Geneva nodded. Ruth had plenty of vodka.

Norton helped Geneva up the steps into the foyer, walked

beside her with his large, warm hand under her elbow.

"One of those boys on bikes knock you down, Miss Geneva? They go fast."

"No, Norton, I was mugged. An attempted mugging I shall call it because they didn't get anything. I kept all my things." She pointed to the purse she carried. Toby had placed the books back on their shelves because Geneva insisted.

"Miss Geneva, you should be seeing a doctor," Norton said.

"All I want is to get into bed and rest."

"I'll bring you lineament from home tomorrow. It makes the sore spots good."

"Thank you. I can use that."

"Miss Ruth? You call her?"

"No, she'll be home soon and I'm fine. No need to worry."

"If you say so, but you call down you need anything." He squeezed her hand, and held open the door for her to enter her apartment. "The foreign folks from the restaurant, they sent a package, waiting for you. Smells nice and spicy. I'll bring it up."

"Thank you. I'll leave the door open and you can set it on the floor."

Once inside, Geneva adjusted the thermostat to warm the apartment because she suddenly felt cold down to her bones. Moving slowly, she filled the tub, poured in Epsom salts, laboriously raised and lowered herself into the hot water. Esther Benmayor was a doctor, or almost, and she'd said nothing was broken but it felt as if every bone had been shaken and moved out of place so they didn't fit right. Soaking and sleep, nourishment from Café Alégria. She'd wake up better in the morning.

What do I know about children's books? Geneva wondered as she lay in bed. She loved seeing the little girls in tutus, running toward their classes in studios along Broadway and Lincoln Center but she knew nothing about children.

Geneva remembered the Russian *Firebird* they went to see for Ruth's first Christmas in America. They rode the bus to the center of town. She was eight and rode next to the window to look out on patches of snow and slush. A troupe from the Sadler Wells Ballet in England was giving a matinee performance of the Columbus Opera House. Ruth told her about the magical Firebird, how a single feather from her head was all a good person needed to have special powers, but how, if anyone bad touched her plumes, they'd go up in flames. When the curtain rose and the red dancer flew on stage, a feather on top of her head, Geneva believed she saw the real Firebird.

Ruth whispered that if Geneva clapped enough, she'd bring the Firebird back after the curtain closed. Geneva pounded her palms together until the curtain opened and the red creature flew across the footlights waving at children in the front seats.

"Dying Swan comes now." Ruth showed Geneva the program. "I saw her die twice in Russia, but Swan was old bird."

When the curtain pulled apart, the stage stayed dark. Then a white, glowing being rose up, arms fluttering, long body shaking and trembling.

"What is wrong with her? Is she going to die?" Geneva could hardly breathe.

"Broken wing," said Ruth, "she must rest."

Finally the white dancer-bird lay down and gave a huge shudder, her feathered head bent over her feet. The clapping sound in Geneva's ears was like an echo of the Swan's heartbeat. Geneva asked again if the swan was dead.

"No, only still resting," said Ruth. "Keep clapping." The swan woman rose up and bowed deeply. Alive! Geneva squeezed Ruth's hand as she never would have squeezed her mother's. Because she wanted the swan back, it stood up and curtsied.

In the final part of the program, Chinese dolls hopped and turned with teacups on their heads. Russian men wearing tall black fur hats leapt straight up in the air with their legs out, then balanced on one hand and spun their bodies around themselves as if their legs were spinning tops. There was a huge woman who hid children under her wide skirts. More and more children came running out until the stage seemed a playground.

Two dancers in blue with turquoise feathers burst onto the stage. The little ballerina wearing blue sequins leapt and her partner soared behind her.

"She is Bluebird," whispered Ruth. "First Firebird, now Bluebird."

Geneva waved and clapped as the Bluebirds flew off, then the Chinese dolls came back running onstage, followed by the children rushing about throwing candy to the audience seated down below. Geneva didn't want any candy or anything to eat. Her eyes, her heart, even her mouth were already bursting with pleasure.

When they left the theater, a cold, wet snow was falling. Geneva's teeth chattered. She remembered her mother saying, "Nothing like Pavlova."

"Better than Soviet swans," Ruth answered.

At home, Ruth made a hot drink with lemon, honey and something spicy like pepper. All night, the dancers whirled in Geneva's head. In the morning, Ruth put a mustard plaster on Geneva's chest.

"She's over-sensitive, with a tendency to hysteria," Geneva heard Celia say. "Let's hope she has more sense than Mama, who didn't stop playing Chopin even when Papa came home for dinner. Sometimes he had to take his own plate from the stove. Because of Chopin, Mama didn't believe her beloved Poles would kill her."

"But Celia, remember, Chopin saved us. We must love Chopin. And Mama."

Only later, Geneva would ask Ruth what she'd meant about Chopin and the Poles. "Mama kept playing for soldiers as Celia and me escaped from window."

For days after the ballet performance, Geneva's fever rose every evening and she wheezed. Celia bought cough syrups and Ruth held cold compresses to her head. When she slept, she dreamed of the princesses and blue birds and swans.

Ruth took Geneva to see her first *Giselle*. The peasant girl, danced by a beautiful dark-haired ballerina named

Alicia Alonso, went mad and became a ghost. Geneva didn't understand. Ruth explained that the girl had made a mistake choosing the nobleman who betrayed her. "Giselle had good village man. Never expect boss's son to marry you. Giselle stupid girl."

"It's not real life." Geneva already knew that ballet wasn't real in the way working for money or cooking or studying at school were real. Ballet was lightness in a world above and outside them, like stars revolving overhead.

Ruth made a borscht for their supper and fed Geneva with a spoon. After two more aspirin, Geneva lay on her good side, trying to get comfortable. Ruth sat in her bra and boxer briefs, sweat damp between her breasts and on her upper lip with its faint mustache, to talk about winter in Siberia and a story that was almost about love, a gift to Geneva lying in pain on her bed.

"Tonight I remember Tatar. I was crazy over Tatar, just crazy."

"A Tatar, like Nureyev?" Geneva asked.

"Shall I tell you story?"

"Of course. I always want to hear everything."

Ruth lit a cigarette.

"I already lived many years in East. War ended sometime, not sure. News comes so slow. Stalin still lives in Moscow, sends more to camps, but Sigi and me—no one cares about two girls. We make repairs on machines, harvest sugar beets, we trade smart. I must transport sugar from co-operative to small airport in Yakutsk for shipping. Middle winter. Airport closed, no flying in storm. We must wait, don't know how long.

"Across hall of airport, I see military officer, Tatar or Caucasus man. Black eyes, mustache, high boots, army fur hat, walks like this." Ruth stood with her beer in hand, strutted to the door and back in her bra and shorts.

"Like Nureyev in boots," Geneva laughed. "Ouch, that hurts."

"Tatar and I, opposite sides of hall, see each other. He is smoking. I am smoking."

Ruth blew her smoke up at the ceiling.

"He watches me. I watch him. He stands, goes to open door behind him. After time, I follow. Inside, darkness. I feel hands on breasts. He lights match and we smoke, eyes can see eyes, like jungle cats. We make love, first and second and third time. Sure big Siberian storm. Three days. Salim goes out, brings back brandy, sausage, choco- late. Name is Salim. Tattoo of Stalin on shoulder. Many men have such tattoos."

After three days, Ruth said, Salim returned from a walk around the airport and told her the storm was let- ting up, that he'd be leaving. Ruth dressed in her coat and boots. After a few minutes, she walked out into the white air or the runways where planes waited. She wasn't sure she saw him before the military cargo plane closed its doors.

"That was Salim, Tatar. We never see each other again. Very big country. Spies everywhere. Salim is officer, Tatar wife, probably ten more children."

"More children?" Geneva was unsure of what she'd

heard, whether it had been an English mistake or something else that Ruth was revealing.

"Tatars have big families." Ruth got up, her back turned.

"You were pregnant, like my mother, from a short time together?" Geneva only guessed this answer that Ruth didn't deny.

"Three days and nights. Strong man. Not surprising. Two months after, I visit woman doctor in Yakutsk. Instruments boiling in water, same pot cooking macaroni for doctor's lunch. Woman's hands hard on me. I don't like woman."

"What happened, Ruth? Did you go through with the abortion?"

Ruth seemed to be lost in that memory of a doctor's office with water boiling on a stove in which macaroni was cooking and sterilizing medical instruments.

"By fall, Jewish Committee in New York sends me first letter from Celia. I can come to America. Only one person, you understand, as during war with Celia."

"My mother was pregnant with me and she got to Switzerland."

Ruth seemed ready to leave the room but Geneva continued.

"My mother didn't get rid of me, Ruth, and I don't think you got an abortion."

"You know nothing. Celia was outside Russia. It was safe to have child in Switzerland. Celia loved Doctor Pavel. You were child of love."

"Thank you, Ruth," Geneva whispered.

Later that night, Geneva couldn't remember if Ruth

had said "it" or "child" or maybe "she" when she spoke of the pregnancy. What if a daughter, a girl conceived in the hardest conditions, was born, and then given to a couple in a Siberian town where Ruth had lived, or given to an orphanage where so many children somehow grew up without parents after the war? If Ruth's daughter survived and lived the past thirty years, she'd be two or three years younger than Geneva. So many times Geneva felt she should be Ruth's daughter and now she felt her intuition was right. She had a phantom sister.

Eight

Anna Pavlova's defense of ballet, published in the 1926 issue of The Dance is a declaration to each new generation of young girls who slip into satin toe shoes and rub their hard points into resin for the first time. "Dancing is pure romance and it is by the grace of romance that man sees himself not as he is but as he should like to be...The dancer wishes to express above all things that surging, rising, uplifted feeling of a great emotion. And so the old masters contrived the technique of the pointed toe to serve as a symbol for the spirit...and when I hear the applause coming up from the darkened house, I feel that perhaps I have given my audience a glimpse of that potent, dazzling beauty, and I know that I have not wasted my life in perfecting the exacting technique of the pointed toe."

Geneva slept some of the day, listening to WBAI, painfully getting up for the bathroom and returning to bed.

She woke to see Connor peering down at her. The first snow must have fallen because a few cool flakes fell on her hot face from his camel hair coat. She felt a delicious chill from the dampness he carried with him.

"It's past time to call truce," Ruth said when she took

Connor's coat and brought a chair. He sat down beside Geneva and took her hand.

"You weren't violated, were you, dear?"

"No, I wasn't." She pointed to her purse in the corner. "All safe and sound."

"Not your things. Your person. You don't look safe and sound."

"I am. What are you doing here so late at night in a storm?" she asked.

"I answered Ruth's call and came right over. Since you haven't published anything damning Rudolf, are we back together?"

Geneva tried to sit up straighter to overcome the disadvantage of lying down, but her right side hurt too much when she moved.

"I haven't written it. After I saw Makarova dance with Nagy, I realized she's back to work, as you said. They heckled her at first but she overcame that as well."

"Who heckled?" he asked.

"I guess Rudi fans. That horrible loud woman with red hair. I didn't see them. I still think someone has to tell the real story but maybe I was too invested."

"Didn't I use those words?"

"It happened as I told you."

"I believe you. It wasn't a question of truth but the consequences. I've heard corroborating accounts since then and I'm open to a revised account. The best might be to write a story or a novel and change the names."

"I don't think I'll ever write it. I've other plans."

"I'm waiting for you to come back."

"Right after this—the mugging—the officers took me back to the dance library. So I could return books I'd taken out. Probably I was in shock and all I could think of was the books that I had to return."

"In your wounded state," Conner shook his head.

"Not that bad. I'd just been there. Justine Delaye was very sweet."

"I know Justine, an authoritative woman, devoted to Martha Graham."

Geneva nodded. "She also suggested I write a book but a different one. I'd introduce children to ballet classics, the way you feel seeing a ballet for the first time,"

"We went to see Firebird, Swan and Bluebird." Ruth carried a tray and teacups.

"All the magical birds Ruth gave me."

"You got sick with excitement. Celia was angry," Ruth said.

"Was your mother an unreachable queen bee?" Connor asked.

Ruth and Geneva looked at each other. Geneva frowned.

"I can't answer that simply, Connor. In Paris, I had a kind of insight that Celia was afraid of losing anyone she might love because it had happened before and she'd been helpless...pregnant during the most awful time, left alone to have a child."

Ruth left the room without listening to the end of Geneva's sentence. She turned and set down cups and a plate. "I bring cakes. Celia, sister, suffered..." She went out with finishing her sentence.

"And so did you, Ruth," Geneva called after her. "But

you stayed resistant to feeling sorry for yourself. I think Celia was always depressed. In other circumstances, she might have been happy to have a little girl who was fanciful but my imagination and my moods pained her. Everything I did rubbed her wrong. I never had a chance to know Celia when I was older. She died when she was only 38 and I wasn't even 18."

"That's tragic," said Connor.

Ruth returned. "Celia has pain in stomach and fever. She turns face to wall and puts her hand over mouth. No doctor, she says, but I call."

"Celia died in the hospital of appendicitis that burst," Geneva said.

"Doctor blamed me," said Ruth.

"You're not responsible for your sister, or your mother, nor for temperamental ballerinas who fail to seduce their partners, whose *amour propre* is on the line," he said.

"Makarova wasn't trying to seduce Nureyev, only get him to partner her the way he should have. And it's not the same thing as with my mother." Geneva squirmed and turned herself until she sat up. "Let's leave it, Connor. Thank you for coming."

"I care for you, silly goose. I want you back. Will you come back if I'm nice?"

"Justine thinks I'll find a publisher. I'm going to write proposals as soon as I can."

"You'll still write for the grown-ups, won't you? If I have to hire another writer, it will be so exhausting. And don't you like good seats at the theater?"

"I do, I appreciate them more than ever." Geneva

winced when she moved. "Am I really such a bargain? Will I get a raise?"

"You do everything so fast, and perfectly. No one else got anything in on time and you only needed editing on a few decisions. I'll pay you more shekels."

"Shekels! What do they translate to?" Geneva only now noticed that the pink from the chill air had left Connor's cheeks and he was very pale, almost white.

"And how are you feeling?" she asked.

"Why should I not be feeling tip top? We all take our cues from the great choreographer. Actually, I'm very cold, deep down."

Connor then did the strangest thing. He climbed into the single bed beside her so they were touching. She tried not to squirm.

"I'm not hurting you?"

"Only certain places. Don't make me laugh, though."

"I feel tired sometimes. How long will the façade hold before I become a ruin, old and mocked?"

"Connor, what's come over you?"

"I'll be 50, ladies," he said. "I'm swearing you to secrecy. No parties."

"50 is nothing, so young," said Ruth.

"Maybe for you, Ruth, but it's not a world for old men like me." He looked at Ruth with his grey eyes and thick long lashes. "I'm going to be a ruin before long."

"You're not anywhere near being old or a ruin, though I've certainly learned that this city is hard on anyone who can't stand up for themselves." Geneva pressed fingers against her mouth. "I'm afraid a few teeth got knocked loose. Those damn boys. They were really young. They should be ashamed."

"I am going to be 50. Moi, who adores beautiful young people. *Icarus* gave me an entrée to pleasure."

"I know that you have higher goals than just vanity," Geneva said.

Connor sighed and fanned himself with Geneva's hankie. "You can wear a man down with your compliments, but don't stop. As dear Oscar put it, 'Experience is the name everyone gives to his mistakes.' I won't make another with you if you promise not to leave me, and also that you'll go to see my doctor."

Connor rose from the bed, patted his pockets as if he thought he might have lost something, leaned over and kissed Geneva's cheek. "I'm happy we made up."

Geneva's shoulder on the side that had gotten pulled still hurt so much she couldn't move. She supposed it was dislocated. "Dancers and athletes dislocate their shoulders. I've heard a single correction puts it back in place," Geneva held out her arm and said, "Pull hard," but Ruth didn't want to.

"You call Albert. He is doctor. He will help."

"But he's in California, at least I think so. How can he help?"

"Call," said Ruth.

Geneva called Stanford Hospital and left a message for Albert Roth.

The phone rang in five minutes.

"Geneva, where are you?"

"I'm at home, in New York. I got mugged but I'm basically all right. I wanted to ask your medical advice if you don't mind."

"Of course I don't mind, but are you sure you're all right? What happened? Were you hit in the head? Did you have a concussion? That can be serious."

"No, not my head. A woman who's had medical training said I don't have broken bones and she cleaned up a few cuts. I think I'm just bruised. I wanted to know if you can displace a shoulder and what to do about it?"

"If you do have a dislocated shoulder, don't wait to see someone. It's painful?"

"I don't have a doctor, Albert. I'm always healthy."

"That's foolish, Geneva. If you wait until I'm off my shift, I'll find someone my father knows in New York and get you a referral for an appointment."

"Thank you. I'm already better talking to you. I'm sorry it took this long to call."

"I've tried to pick up the phone and tell you how stupid I felt, how stupid I still feel, about leaving London without saying goodbye."

"I've wanted to call to say the same thing. It was my fault. My head got turned by everything that happened."

"I read your interview with Rudi. You were so close up that I felt jealous. I can understand better why I wasn't the center of attention."

"It wasn't him. It was all that happened. My foolish enthusiasms."

"Those enthusiasms are what's wonderful about you. You're so intense."

"To a fault," she said.

"When I saw you in London, you looked changed," he said.

"It was cosmetic, a brilliant hairdresser."

"When you didn't come to meet me in the lobby the way you said you would, I got it into my mind you were meeting another man."

"No, not at all. I thought I'd explain to Makarova who sent me away. It was awful. And then not finding you. I looked everywhere that night, the next day. I kept expecting we'd find each other. I dreamed we were always missing each other."

"I'd come from the airport right to the theater. I hadn't even found a hotel for the night. I made an assumption...."

"Of course."

"I decided you weren't coming to me so I collected my things from the coat check and took a cab to Heathrow. Once I got on a flight, I realized I could have called St. John and found out where you were staying. I got home and had another all-nighter on rotation, time just passed. I never stopped wanting to call."

"I went into nearly every pub around Covent Garden the next day. I got to know the neighborhood quite well."

"I have a break in my rotation in two weeks. Shall I come to New York?"

"Really, you mean it? You'd put up with me again?"

"If you get us tickets for another beautiful evening,

I will come. I'll give you a referral to a colleague of my father's. She'll fix your shoulder right up."

———————

Albert's referral, Dr. Reta Shah, moved Geneva's shoulder with one painful maneuver back into position and stabilized her loose tooth. "Why did you wait so long. Do you choose to suffer, young woman?"

"I thought it would get better."

"I'm glad you came to see me. You have a strong will. Not always helpful."

When she tried to pay, Dr. Shah shook her head. "It's all taken care of. And I've got some cover-up for those bruises."

Dr. Shah spread a cool liquid across Geneva's forehead, massaged it into her cheeks. They waited, then the doctor handed Geneva a mirror.

"You are a miracle worker. Now I know where to come for anything. Can I at least take you out to lunch? Maybe a ballet when I have tickets."

"I'd like that, thank you. I never get to the ballet. Remember not to lift anything for a week. You'll want to be careful with the shoulder. You'll heal quickly." The doctor sighed. "Oh, to be young again like you."

"I'll be 32 this summer."

"You're a baby," answered the doctor.

Geneva now saw that Dr. Reta Shah was an old woman with grey under a reddish dye in her cropped hair and hands, still strong enough to put a shoulder back in place, wrinkled and spotted. Geneva wished she could ask Dr. Shah about Albert and his family and how she should be with him, but the doctor smiled and showed her out.

———————

A half hour after Geneva arrived home from the doctor, Geneva realized the worst pain was over. She could move carefully and feel almost normal. She was in time for a WBAI evening concert of Sephardic music from Spain that made her think of Esther wielding her frying pan so effectively. As the singer's vibrato rose with hot joy and fell in peals, Geneva imagined fountains in Granada only seen in photographs. Why not take time and travel with Ruth? She sat down to listen more attentively. The elegiac music recalled a passage she'd read about art transforming the bitter taste of suffering. She felt eager to get to the library and begin work. She'd start with *The Nutcracker* because so many children knew it, then go on to *The Sleeping Beauty,* then *Swan Lake.* If Justine was right, she'd help Ruth with their expenses, and they could take the trip.

Telling children stories of the ballets, she wouldn't spare them the thrills or the terrors. Ballets were dark as the darkest fairy tales—being kidnapped by an evil magician, tormented by violent rat kings, stuck by poisoned spindles, haunted by ghostly brides—but in the end, the most threatening stories gave way to Sugar Plums and redemption so children could sleep with good fairies in their heads.

Nine

The Sleeping Beauty, Marius Petipa's choreographic masterpiece based on Charles Perrault's fairy tale and set to Tchaikovsky, debuted at the Marynsky Theater, St. Petersburg, in 1890. The longest classical ballet and often the costliest for companies to mount—Diaghilev's Ballets Russes went broke presenting it in London in 1921—is a cream puff of formal duets, the ballerina a rose in virginal pink organza wooed by the prince in white and silver tunic, while witty character dances and dramatic battles between the good Lilac Fairy and the bad Carabosse are its real delights. Children never forget the Chinese Teacups, Puss and Boots, the Blue Birds, and Mother Ginger, whose great skirts release a dozen little dancers. Trust Mathew Bourne to create a version of the classic that darkens the fairy tale: in Bourne's Sleeping Beauty: a Gothic Romance, Prince Désiré is turned into a vampire who must stay alive long enough to waken Princess Aurora at the end of her 100-year sleep.

Geneva showered, washed her hair and brushed until it spun out around her shoulders. She covered remaining bruises with the makeup. She was almost ready when the buzzer sounded. She rushed back into her bedroom to smooth the cover on the bed and lined up magazines on the table in the living room.

Albert had shaved his beard and looked younger, like a student.

"We keep surprising each other. No longer the young Freud," she said.

"You are so intuitive."

"You're not going into psychiatry?"

"You're not 100% intuitive but before I say anything else, if it's not too much trouble, I could use a coffee and a quick shower. I hate the red-eye but it's convenient."

She directed him to the bathroom, gave him a towel and went to the kitchen. When he came up behind her, his hands were wet. She stepped away and he dropped his towel. She leaned down to retrieve it, to cover him up, but before she could, he took it from her hands and stood naked before her.

"Albert," she said, backing into the stove, her eyes down. "Aren't we going to talk?"

He slid his hand up and down her hip. "You tell me if something hurts unbearably?"

"Nothing's unbearable." She tried to avoid looking at his erection but he took her head between his hands and held it steady so she saw for the first time what she'd seen from a distance, clothed, contained in dance belts, including Nureyev's famed cod piece. This was all flesh, darkish red, all flesh and seemed to look at her.

"Anything that hurts," he repeated, pulling her toward him, "you'll say so. I've been thinking of this since we met. Don't be afraid."

"It's not the bruises," she managed to whisper. "I've never had a lover."

"I wondered. I will treat you as a sacred trust. I promise the girl you still are that you will be happy today."

Before she could shake her head at his speech, he stepped back and raised two fingers in the *Swan Lake* sign of true love forever, which made them both laugh. He lifted her up, carried her across the living room and into her bedroom where he placed her on her bed and began to unbutton her blouse. If anything hurt, Geneva's resistance to pain gave way to the wonder of touch, the waves of pleasure his hands sent through her. At just the right moment, she was sure she heard the bells of Saint John the Divine though she might only be imagining because the church was miles away.

"No more beard." Geneva stroked his smooth cheek. "Tell me why."

"The beard I had," he brought her hand to his cheek, "that beard gave a paternal impression."

"Freud?" she asked.

He nodded. "Freud, whereas the mind I most admire is Jung because he embraces the female as well as the male principle. I'm leaving Stanford before the end of my residency. It's too rigid and run by Freudian analysts like my father who think they are god. I'm going to start from fresh, beginning a residency under a woman supervisor in La Jolla, in southern California. I know I'll find my place there."

"That sounds untraditional." She snuggled closer, breathing in his warmth.

"Enough to give my mother and father fits, but my choice feels right. I've always admired Jung, and Joseph Campbell and Levi Strauss. I'm turning 26 this November. I feel I'm really starting my life now. You've had an amazing influence on me, Geneva."

"Me? But how? I don't know anything about psychiatry." She pulled the sheet up to her nose. She hadn't known his age, that he was still in his twenties. I'm not exactly a maternal figure, she thought. Or perhaps I am, formerly an older virgin.

"You didn't make fun of my feminine, emotional side when we met at the ballet in San Francisco. I hoped we'd become lovers in London but you were indifferent. I even saw you as leading me on and betraying me like the Black Swan."

"I wasn't. I'm sorry about that. Everything conspired against our being together."

"In our culture, a boy can't love ballet and be a real man," he said. "I wanted to prove to you that I am, a man."

She took his hand and brought theirs together to her lips. "You are, but I have to confess that when we met in San Francisco, you were so emotional in the middle of *Swan Lake*, I was guessing that you were homosexual."

"You see, these are the misconceptions I live with." Albert leaned back in the bed with his hands behind his head. "My mother was always trying to arrange something for me as if it were a test. She was fixing me up with a date when I met you. Remember, you were wearing a red carnation and so was I."

"I had a rose. The doorman at the hotel had given

me a rose when I was leaving for the ballet. He probably thought I looked drab."

"Mother had given me the flower to identify a young woman she'd picked out for me. It just didn't turn out to be the same person she had in mind. Thank heavens for cosmic mistakes."

Cosmic? She wondered. The mistaken red flowers seemed more like comedy.

She turned on her side to get off her still-sore shoulder, "I remember wondering about the intended woman with the red carnation."

———

After they'd eaten a sandwich Geneva prepared, they made love again. This time she kept her eyes open and shared with him the delight she felt.

"Geneva, everything is meant to be." He stroked her forehead, her ears.

"I guess that's true in a way. The thugs gave me bruises that brought you here." She was teasing him but he wasn't to be side-tracked.

"It's more than that. I've had a few trips and I will take more," he said.

"Trips? You came to England. Sorry, again, sorry, but now you're here. I like the idea that you take trips."

"No I mean another kind of trip. It's what's called taking psychedelic drugs. You've heard of LSD. That's a synthetic formulation but there are naturally occurring hallucinogens that come from plants. I'm going on a vision quest in Mexico before I begin my study in La

Jolla. Not alone. I wouldn't feel safe yet. It's a group of incoming students. We'll be eating magic mushrooms. I hope one day you'll share the experience with me in the desert, or perhaps the jungle." He smiled a far-away smile. "You have visions of beauty like the ballet but this is more, much more. With your sensitivity, everything you see thereafter will be enhanced. When you go to a ballet like *Giselle*, and you're watching the Wilis in the forest at night, it will be you there yourself."

Geneva pulled away and covered herself.

"I don't want to be in a forest having visions, Albert. The dark night in Paris was crazy enough. I'm a cautious person. I have no knowledge of drugs. I like sitting at a distance and watching. I've always been that way."

"You will never know until you've tried what you might be. There's a heaven to be explored beyond our limited senses."

"With heaven, there's always hell, Albert." Her voice rose and she felt herself trembling with some kind of fear of the unknown. "Drugs are not for me."

"There's no need to be afraid. You weren't afraid of this, were you?" he stroked her hair. "We're only beginning our journey here, Geneva. This is a first step. We have far to go. You will release your inhibitions and see through the veil of illusions."

"I like veils, and tulle. What do you mean about inhibitions? I didn't feel I was inhibited just a short time ago." Give me a little credit, she thought.

Albert kissed her. "That was lovely as only an innocent and a pure person can be, which is what I love about you, but we can go further, so much further. I always made distinctions that divided me from my true, androgynous self—the one my mother doesn't accept, but that's another story. We're all androgynous if we dare explore it."

"Albert, what does this all mean? Are you going to experiment with wearing a ballet tutu? You've seen the Trocadero ballerinas?"

"I don't mean so literally. Actually, I don't know what I'll do or what will happen except I've never been so excited about the future and expanding my consciousness beyond this puny here and now." He laughed. "Uh oh, not so puny. Come closer."

Geneva was happy that Albert's erection ended the conversation.

———

She woke up looking at her watch. "Ruth will be home soon. She's been gone a long time, as if she knew you were here and she left us alone."

"If your Ruth is as open to vibrations as I think she is, she knows," he said.

"Oh Albert, isn't it more likely she came in quietly and heard us? I mean, isn't there a rational explanation? Anyway, she's bound to be back."

"Don't fall into doubt, darling. She will want to share experiences with us."

"No, I don't think so, Albert. She's hard-headed, very practical, and she wouldn't interject herself in my life. I'm her niece." Geneva started to get up when Albert pulled her back.

"Don't leave me without telling me your feelings right now. Are you happy?"

"Well, I am, but this stuff about trips bothers me. I've gotten to travel to London and Paris. That's my idea of trips. My life isn't as flexible as you somehow imagine. I've been given an opportunity to write books. I'll need the library in New York."

"There a connection between us, Geneva, don't deny it. We're attuned."

"I acknowledge that but I don't understand a lot of what you've been saying."

"It takes time and you will."

They heard the key turning in the door followed by steps. "Home!" Ruth called.

Ruth worked a half-day on Saturdays and then did the week's shopping but it was almost dark now, so surely, Geneva thought, she'd waited to come home.

They hurried to dress and greet Ruth who gave them knowing smiles and suggested they go out to eat because they must be hungry. Ruth winked at Geneva.

On the street, Albert linked arms between them, one tall young man between two short women.

La Casa Alégria was candle lit, fragrant with limes and curry spices.

"You are recovered." Esther hugged Geneva and then Ruth. "You have brought your friend, the doctor?"

"How did you know I'm a doctor?" Albert asked.

Esther shrugged, smiled. "I just thought perhaps..."

"You see, doubting Geneva, how people really know things without being told."

"Yes, the doctor is here from San Francisco. Albert, this Esther and her husband, Moise, my saviors," said Geneva.

"Boyfriend," said Ruth with a wink. Geneva blushed.

"*Mazel tov*, children," said Esther.

"Be at home here." Moise directed them to a table.

They ordered the spicy prawns, a chicken curry in coconut milk, heaping mounds of rice, a yogurt dip, dishes of tangy black beans and fried plantains.

"Wonderful!" Ruth pronounced at each taste. "They are international cooking."

"Boundaries are in the mind's eye," said Albert.

"They come from Cuba and India. They met in Israel on a kibbutz." Geneva felt the need to be precise where Albert seemed to favor the general and vague.

"Esther's home was Kerala in South India, a very old Jewish community," Moise told them. Esther came up behind her husband and rested her hand on his shoulder. Her smooth brown hand was damp and her nails pink and cut short.

"There weren't young men in Cochin. They sent me to Israel to find a husband."

"And so she did find me," Moise placed his arm around her waist.

"Our first, Benjamin, was born here. He is total American," said Esther.

Benny arrived with chilled mangoes topped by finely sliced limes for dessert.

"The world is one," Albert smiled and closed his eyes. Was he happy tasting the sweet mangoes or had he taken some sort of pill that made him smile all the time? Geneva wondered.

———————

By the third morning of his visit, so many of Albert's clothes lay scattered on Geneva's floor and bathroom that the two rooms, her bedroom and the living room, didn't seem big enough to contain them. His shirts, underwear, and socks seemed to cover every surface; no matter how often she picked them up, they returned to make a kind of obstacle course to getting around the apartment. The way he moved about, swinging long arms and legs, made papers fly from her work table, as if she were hosting some kind of primate. He took books from the shelves, browsed a moment and left them opened face down. She hadn't realized how much she liked books closed and papers that lay at right angles on surfaces. He knocked against a figurine of a ballerina that Geneva watched fall. One of her favorites, part of the stage set from Connor, tumbled, but luckily it was wood and didn't break. She began moving breakables out of Albert's range of motion.

The last day of Albert's visit, they made love in the morning before he dressed for his flight. *Among the ruins*, she said to herself as she stroked his thick black hair.

"I'll miss you and your dear auntie," he said.

"And I'll miss you. She did share our being together, in her way."

"We're getting closer and closer to real sharing of ourselves with others."

"Albert, who do you think we are going to share with?

I mean, Ruth looks kindly on us, and I'm sure she hopes you'll return. Is there something else you mean?"

"Sharing love so it encompasses more than us," he said.

"Not physical love?" She shook her head. "I don't understand."

"You'll have to read the books I'll send you, one particularly by Norman O. Brown. It's revolutionary, or rather, it goes back to our true beginnings, our polyamorous state, polyandry as the anthropologists call it about primitive peoples, who weren't primitive at all. It must have been Edenic, really a paradise of love. This great writer has moved to California and I hope to meet him when I'm ready."

"I don't have anything to say if you're saying what I think you are, some kind of group thing like I've heard about, especially in California. I don't like leaving civilization."

"We'll get you used to new ideas, darling."

"Not this morning. You don't want to miss the plane."

He smiled his goofy, appealing smile as if missing a plane was something that didn't matter in the larger picture he always saw, but she hustled him out the door.

"I'll take you to get the shuttle so you don't get lost, but I have to go to the library."

———

When Ruth asked that evening, "Do you miss young man? I like Albert but he leaves mess everywhere."

"I know," said Geneva. "You have to pick up after him like a baby. I'll miss him but I couldn't live with him under the same roof for even a week."

"What happens then?" asked Ruth.

"I don't know. It was wonderful in some ways but a lot of trouble in others. He couldn't live in New York and I'm not going to California."

"Now you are woman," Ruth said, "Different choices."

"Don't say that!" Geneva hurried to her room and slammed the door before she burst into tears. I do love him, she cried into her pillow, but he's impossible.

Part Four

Ten

Every aspiring ballerina dreams the Nutcracker Prince will carry her to the land of snowflakes and sugar plums, but in recent years, even the venerable Nutcracker, like Swan Lake, has undergone reconstruction. During the Christmas holidays the score is recognizably Tchaikovsky, while the choreography and libretto are anything but. Les Ballets Trocaderos de Monte Carlo, an all-male troupe dancing Nutcracker, prompted a reviewer to ask, "Who is that handsome ballerina?" Mark Morris' Hard Nut, set in the 1960s, opens with the kids in front of TV and men wearing tutus. In The Cracked Nut, from the Philippines, a young girl confronts colonialism rather than the Rat King.

Geneva's work place became her reserved cubicle in the library of the New York Center for the Performing Arts at Lincoln Center where temperatures stayed regulated and lights glowed after darkness fell outside. She had access to film clips and research materials, worked all day and was kept going by coffee and bagels the librarians shared during breaks. Her 1976 New Year's gift was a contract for *Christmas Eve and The Nutcracker*. The advance made Ruth gasp.

"For children, this much money?"

"Some we save for our trip, to see Europe. Maybe to Russia," Geneva said.

Ruth frowned. "Why? Nothing to see in Russia."

Perils of the Swan Princess followed in six months. Geneva called Odette a princess rather than a queen because little girls loved princesses who were young like themselves, while queens were sometimes not-so-helpful mothers. The illustrator drew Odile, the Black Swan, like a negative photographic image of Odette, as if the enchanted princess had gone from sunlight to night, becoming her own shadow under a shivery sliver moon, which was how Geneva imagined her, with the delicacy of Makarova and the intense seduction of Plisetskaya. Illustrations for the Black Swan had glitters affixed to her wings on the page.

When the *Times* recommended *Perils of the Swan Princess* in the holiday book children's pages, sales took off. "Accuracy, beauty, and charm for readers of many ages," the *Times'* and *Publisher's Weekly* wrote. Connor insisted on giving the book party at the Tea Room, reminiscing that he'd discovered Geneva just up from the provinces.

The librarians, Justine, Toby and especially Francis, who wore a burgundy velvet evening jacket, were made a great fuss over by Connor. "Denishawn, those were the days of my extreme youth," Connor said. "You were next to the gods and not outshone by them." It seemed Francis might faint and had to be held up by Justine. Geneva herself, feeling such relief at completing work everyone seemed to like, drank enough champagne to see the red lamps on the tables double, like Japanese lanterns bobbing on water. Ruth and Connor lifted her under the arms and walked her out into a starry night.

The next two volumes, *Sleeping Beauty* and *Giselle*, were already laid out in her mind while she added to a separate folder, *The Russians Who Leaped West*, with all the material on Nureyev and Makarova she'd never published, notes after seeing young Mikhail Baryshnikov and the continuing career of Maya Plisetskaya. Plisetskaya wasn't a defector—she'd stayed with the Bolshoi all her life—but Geneva saw her fierce independence, risky involvement in politics and experimental ballets as a leap beyond Soviet censors.

Late on a January night, Connor called and, as if reading from a telegram, hoarsely said, "Deadline stop. Situation desperate stop. Taxi waiting stop."

Geneva looked at the bedside clock. "It's midnight. Ruth has to get up to work tomorrow and I'm in bed."

"I've sent a taxi."

The taxi was waiting and sped her through intersecting avenues of the Park. When Geneva arrived, she found Connor examining two photographs with a magnifying glass. "Take a look." Connor thrust black and white photos at her. In the first, a woman on toe with impossibly long legs, glared into the camera. The second, in profile, showed a small catlike head, the sweep of black brows and eye shadow almost a mask.

"Odile gone feral?" Geneva asked.

"Katya K. Pictures are appearing all over Europe of Katya mingling with Saudi royals and the demi-monde, a super star, a female Nureyev, surpassing Plisetskaya."

"That's ridiculous, Connor. Plisetskaya is the whole artist not just legs."

Connor rattled the photos. "If we can get to her, we've got a scoop and god knows we need it. I'm waiting for you to dig up news because this Miss Kitty is a blank slate."

"This person could also be a Soviet fiction to make us look foolish. You can't afford mistakes." Geneva did not want to use the word *bankrupt*.

"Success has given you a hard shell, Geneva. I hardly recognize the willing girl I knew. Just because you're on the ascendant, I hope you don't forget your origins, even if I look like an old molting bird."

Geneva noticed that Connie's black curls were thinning and when he bent his head down, she saw a bald spot. Even his brooding brows weren't as thick.

"You're not running off to California to bed that lad in San Francisco," Connor said. "Ruth keeps me apprised. Has he fallen out of favor?"

"Oh Connie, stop. Albert is in thrall to the female principle in general and a Russian woman, a doctor, in particular. Somehow we've devolved into confidantes though it's always about him. All I have to do is listen to his dramatic life."

"Isn't that what you've always done? You're not getting any younger either."

"That's unkind, Connor. Maybe it's true. I haven't

planned to be alone. Albert tells me that his Russian has a golden aura. My aura is probably muddled, brown and wears glasses. I could do with less confidential material. But I may go to San Francisco to see Makarova later this year. He would like that. You wouldn't pay my expenses."

Connor patted the seat beside him. "You know I'm sorry that love hasn't worked out for either of us. It's a shame we didn't marry, you and I."

"You're joking."

"Not entirely." He took her hand.

"I could have married you for the money, when you had it."

"You're such a balanced person. Cupid is so unfair. Did you really believe I was handsome in my youth?"

"You were too handsome for your own good."

"Do you know I also gave some thought to marrying Ruth. I like older women."

"Can I tell her that? How about a ménage a trios?" As Geneva teased, she recalled with a moment of vertigo Albert's wish for more than a trio, maybe a dozen people all writhing around somewhere in a jungle. What an impossible hope, that she would ever find a common understanding with him. Yet she still loved him, not with a desire for possession but deep longing that was going to remain unfulfilled.

"Now that sounds interesting. What a night we've had, and before you go, I need you to look at my favorite painting in the inner sanctum."

"You don't mean the Monet?"

"Darling, Monsieur Monet has been gone for months

and he *never* graced the inner sanctum. A Japanese owns Monet now. Monet was *Orientalist* by nature."

"I thought Jeff took the painting to Sasha's to be cleaned."

"He did, and there it stayed. Water lilies were Mother's taste anyway. I was never in love with them. Now I'm talking about a truly heartbreaking loss. Come look at my beloved Bacchus who leaves home tomorrow with Sasha of the golden curls."

Connor laughed until he started coughing.

"Are you all right?" she asked.

"Let's not talk about me. Come." He took her hand and led her to the bedroom. The unmade bed lay buried in a tangle of sheets and clothes. Shoes and pants were strewn around on the carpet, reminding her of Albert during his stay but Connor was always so neat and fastidious.

"I've never been in the inner sanctum. Where's your housekeeper?" she asked.

"Economies everywhere. Look at the lips." Connor leaned close to a large canvas so his head was in the way as if he were going to deliver a kiss on the cherry red mouth of a boy she now saw. The strange and beautiful face was painted white as a Geisha.

"Bacchus is overripe, wouldn't you say?" he asked.

"What a painting, Connor. Is it Caravaggio? I mean, is it a real one?"

"He's capable of great corruption," said Connor. "Bacchus, like Rudolf Nureyev, has mellowed into a less threatening figure over the years, has he not?"

"Yes, I suppose he has," Geneva agreed. "I'm hearing Nureyev isn't well."

"Always ignore gossip, or rather, leave it to me. Now my Bacchus here is without passport. I mean, the boy, the painting, never had provenance, and being illegal, he was a risky investment from the moment I saw him, but I couldn't resist. I wake up to him every day and say good morning to my illegitimate son. Since I've had him as well authenticated as an illegal immigrant can be, he's going out for greedy eyes to look on."

Geneva stepped closer. "For all these years, Connor, you've been admiring yourself from the bed. You resemble each other, you know that. The muscular legs, short but well-defined."

"Did you know I wore lifts in my shoes?"

"No, I didn't."

"I fooled most people. Go on. And don't tell me I'm doing a Dorian Gray, that would be too obvious."

"The lower third of the painting, the basket with spotted, bruised fruit rests on the table—that's where time's indignities are showing first. Higher up, your boy-god's seductive eyes promise the eternal present but of course, the doors of hell await."

"You're so good."

"It's been a long time since I've practiced taking home a painting. When Ruth and I first moved to New York, we went to museums all the time, and since we had no money and blank walls, we decorated by taking a painting home in our minds, memorizing all the details. I'm now seeing the full wine glass in one hand, the black mask in the other. Is Bacchus celebrating a last supper? There's so many hidden clues, so much going on."

Connor stood staring. "I count on your discretion and your memory for recalling him when he's no longer here. I think the evening has been long enough for me."

"You called me at midnight." She looked at her watch. "It's now two." She took Connor's hand that felt hot and dry. They stood without speaking as Geneva tried to take in more of the painting.

"I also count on you to insist on an epitaph from Wilde on my gravestone. What do you think? 'History is merely gossip.'"

"I think that you won't need an epigraph anytime soon,"

"Epitaph," he corrected.

"I understand," she said. "Why are you so morbid?"

"Losing Bacchus, I suppose. Take the photos I showed with you. And give my love to Ruth."

———————

The next morning, Geneva asked Ruth to examine the photographs of Katya K.

"Connor thinks she's the new female Nureyev. You think so?" she asked Ruth.

Ruth laughed. "I think Miss Kitty here is guy. Is Connie losing grip?"

"I'm worried about him. I think he's aware, too. For now, if we can save him from major embarrassment that will be good. If you'd talk with him, he'll listen."

Eleven

Anthony Tudor's Lilac Garden premiered in London in 1936. Commentators have read the story of the frustrated, socially repressed woman to have been about love that dared not say its name. Whatever his subtext, Tudor gave several generations of dramatic ballerinas—Nora Kaye, Lynn Seymour, Natalia Makarova—a chance to dance Caroline, a character more complex than a swan princess. Before they stepped on the stage in a blue ruffled dress, Tudor instructed each dancer to get inside Caroline, "Smell the lilacs, feel and express the intensity of her emotions."

A s the house lights dimmed upon the San Francisco Opera House, a tall figure in black stood in the aisle beside Geneva.

"The lady is alone?"

When their shoulders touched, the current Geneva felt pass between them seemed to connect her not only to Albert now but to that first meeting in this theater six years earlier. How strange it was. They were no longer involved, had not seen each other for two years during which time he'd talked about his Russian love, and yet they were still connected by whatever force brought them together in the beginning. Albert now lived with Anna and sent Geneva postcards from places like Bali, Pondicherry, and Tangiers where they traveled for spiritual quests and yoga retreats. Geneva had had no lovers since Albert. When he completed his training as a Jungian therapist, she sent him an expensive edition of *The Archetypes and the Collective Unconscious*. The book seemed perfect for a respected friend. Now he'd flown up from southern California for two ballet nights.

He whispered, "I watched you come in and then I waited. Lovely suit."

"I retrieved my London costume." She didn't say she'd been dieting and attending exercise classes at the 92nd Street Y—for overall health and postponing middle age spread, nothing especially to do with him, though she'd been working out harder lately.

"Your beard is back but it's smaller. What are we supposed to understand?"

"You see the beard as a symbol, that's interesting. Should I open a therapy practice on my own, do you think?"

"Of course you should."

"Anna's father's Russian oil so we won't starve the first years when I'll be establishing a practice."

Before Geneva could respond, the conductor stepped into the orchestra pit and the violinist tapped his bow. The curtain rose on the twilight setting of *Lilac Garden*.

"May I hold your hand? I feel we're connected," he said.

Geneva closed her fingers around his as Natalia Makarova entered wearing a pale blue dress with a ruffle at the hem. A young man in uniform swept in, bowed crisply before he crushed her against his chest. She swooned in that utterly abandoned way Geneva remembered, Odette in white giving herself to love, Giselle lost to the world.

Geneva felt the heated passion, and the bitter regret as Caroline was forced by convention to accept an older husband. In the final scene, friends made an arch under which the girl in blue and the unloved man took resigned steps toward marriage.

"Times have changed, but I think it holds up," Geneva said as Makarova stepped before the curtain to receive huge bouquets. "It's the kind of personal role Makarova was begging for. I'm happy for her."

"Families still don't understand we must be free to make our own choices," Albert said. "They can't let go of us."

"I've had a different experience, as you know. My family is Ruth and she wants me to be independent. Are your parents still here in San Francisco?"

"Yes, and my mother has requested lunch with you. She says she's been waiting for years and has reserved a table at Trader Vic's for tomorrow."

"Albert, that's flattering but I can't have lunch tomorrow. Makarova has agreed to see me sometime during the day and I have to wait for her call. Then I'm moving over to Berkeley for Plisetskaya's performance in the evening, where you'll join me."

"My mother is putting herself out. She's a very respected ballet donor."

"Thank you, but I'm going to wait to hear from Makarova."

"I thought you'd make yourself free one time for something I ask of you."

He turned away, seeming to sulk. She could squeeze his hand for friendship or reproach but she let it go and folded her own

"I'm sorry. I had no idea. What about Anna? Is she here also?"

"Mother is not in favor of Anna and has made it clear she thinks there too much trouble ahead with the Russian background."

"But if you love each other, you'll do what you want, not what they say, won't you? After so much exploration, the experiments you've been through together. I imagine Anna is brave and a good partner for you, Albert."

"Won't you meet Mother tomorrow, as a favor to me?"

"Anytime but tomorrow." Geneva took a deep breath. "I don't see where I fit into this role, Albert. Really, you're lacking some kind of intuition here. I can send your mother the boxed set of my children's books that's coming out for Christmas. Maybe for her grandchildren, but I don't even know if you have brothers or sisters and if they have children, that's how little I know about you, Albert."

"You don't give anything freely, do you? I thought you'd broken from St. John."

"Broken? Like broken up? That didn't happen because we weren't together that way. You always knew that he was gay. He was my mentor, he gave me my chance.

Connor isn't well and *Icarus* is in hiatus, but he and I are still close. I'm here on my own dime for my new book, and I get to see you."

"You never stop working on deadlines and just let yourself live."

Geneva stiffened in her seat. "Albert, please, let's not disagree about what we can't resolve. I never asked where Anna comes from in Russia."

"Irkutsk, Siberia. She loves ballet but grew too tall to dance, they told her."

"Irkutst? Ruth was in Yakutsk, I guess they're not close. Siberia's huge, isn't it? I want to know about that place when she was there, to do some family research."

"What is this about? You've never told me anything about Ruth's past."

"It's dramatic and it's also vague because she keeps it that way. Ruth told me she got pregnant during a three-day storm with a man she never saw again. She says she had an abortion because she was still a political exile. But I suspect she didn't go through with the abortion and that she gave up that baby for adoption in Siberia. She denies it. Her child would be about my age now, close to 40, grown up in very hard conditions. She'd be my first cousin. For some reason, I feel she's more like a sister."

"A soul sister you mean?"

"I don't know, perhaps yes. Certainly different but maybe alike. I mean, I guess I want to understand about myself, too. This mystery person might help, and I'd help her."

"Because she's a spiritual double." Albert now looked

concerned and attentive. "I find this extraordinary. I'm sure Anna will try to find some birth records."

"Thank you." Geneva took Albert's hand. "And please tell your mother I'm free anytime after tomorrow. I'll be in Berkeley but I can come back to San Francisco."

"I'll tell her. Do you think I attach too much importance to Mother's opinions?"

"I didn't say that."

"But I do. I'm not completely clear of my shackles," he said.

The lights dimmed and Makarova came on stage wearing the sheer white tunic of Terpsicore in George Balanchine's *Apollo*. Her fine legs and feet moved with the precision beloved by Balanchine, while her arms and her back expressed her unique line.

"She's wonderful as a mature dancer, better than ever. I can't wait to see Plisetskaya," Geneva said softly to Albert.

———————

The next morning, Geneva took a cab to the Marina where the sun was shining on the masts of boats anchored and tied along the Bay. Further out, their sails tipped and leaned into a firm breeze, and in the distance, the hollowed outlines of the Golden Gate Bridge glowed red through low puffy clouds.

She walked up a flight of steps, and rang the bell. An extremely tall, pale man with black hair slicked like wax and skin pulled tightly over high cheekbones answered at the first ring. He made a small bow and listened when she said she had an appointment with Natalia Makarova.

"Yes, my wife is expecting you. Please follow me," he said.

Geneva blushed at her thought that this specter-like person was a butler or an usher for a late-night horror movie.

The sunken living room, pale and bright, overlooked the San Francisco Bay. At the center of the room, beside a pale pink and cream floral display, sat Natalia Makarova on an Empire-style sofa. She wore a floor-length mulberry dress the color of a cloudy sunset whose folds of cloth came together in a gold pin on one shoulder. An ivory crocheted shawl trailed over her arms. An exquisite miniature, Geneva thought, in its gold setting. She regretted not having a camera and remembered she'd wanted one at the first interview in the Mayflower Hotel.

As soon as Makarova began speaking, Geneva's apprehension that she'd be remonstrated vanished. She suspected she wasn't even remembered.

"You met my husband?" she asked.

"Yes. Thank you for seeing me. I loved your *Lilac Garden* last night, and you danced Balanchine wonderfully. You were perfect in both."

Makarova acknowledged the compliment with a slight smile.

"Are there still roles or particular characters that you still wish to dance?"

The ballerina exhaled smoke from her cigarette in its long holder. "Of course. There's Russian saying, everyone goes crazy in own way. Two types of women go mad. The first type, simple woman, like Ophelia and Giselle—we call them *blue heroines* in Russia. Other, like Nastasya Philipovna in Dostoevsky. In *Idiot,* you know Nastasya?" Makarova didn't wait for Geneva's answer and then said, "Nastasya other type, doesn't know why she destroys what she loves."

"Do you think she's like Odile?" Geneva asked.

Makarova smoked. "Odile lives in kind of chaos, like Nastasya Philipovna. You know poem 'Unknown Woman', Alexander Blok?"

Geneva shook her head. "No, I'm sorry that I don't."

"I give bad translation from Russian but poem says woman enters restaurant with feather boa, glass in hand. Woman is eternal mystery and melancholy."

"Will you dance with Mikhail Baryshnikov? Did you have any idea beforehand that he was going to defect from the Kirov?"

"Absolutely. He plans from time I defect. Like me, no interest in politics. Everything with Misha is intuitive, like me. We will dance, will be true art."

Geneva counted three cigarettes that the ballerina lit, partially smoked and snuffed out. Smoking seemed a sensual act for Makarova, as if drawing it in and out brought threads of memory together in her mind.

"I am not afraid when I trust partner. I have common language. You maybe think of Rudolf? He is not such a gentleman, but he is artist. You see, there are always risks. Risks are artist's life. Risk necessary to art. Everything you live shows in art."

"I wanted to apologize for many years ago..."

The tall dark husband appeared on the landing above the living room. He tapped his watch. Geneva hadn't asked all she'd have liked to but there had been a willingness in Makarova, a confidence that gave an opening once again.

From the moment the cello notes of Saint-Saens concerto for *The Dying Swan* began, Geneva wanted to tell Albert how surprised she was that Maya Plisetskaya, the prima ballerina *assoluta*, grandest of great dancers, was opening her program with the old chestnut. She smiled, remembering Ruth's comment, 'old Soviet swans' though Plisetskaya's trembling *pas de bourrées* back and forth across the dark stage was ageless, an embodiment of a soul fighting to the end. Slowly lowering herself to the stage, arms mourning her own mortality, this swan defied death with all her forces.

"Isn't she magnificent?" Geneva squeezed Albert's hand. He nodded. Applause and bravos from the orchestra to the top of Zellerbach Hall lasted longer than the ballet itself. The audience rose to its feet and demanded more curtain calls until finally the ballerina was laughing and clapping so hard herself the theater quieted again.

Geneva consulted the program. "Wow, we'll see parts of *Anna Karenina*. Plisetskaya's husband wrote the score." When the dance began, Geneva marveled at the ballerina's choice in a young partner, Alexandr Godunov, tall, blond, and sullen, a preening Count Vronsky who pursued the object of his passion with a certain diffidence, leaving no doubt that he'd soon tire of the older woman. When the ballerina reached out for her lover, Geneva saw the artistry of Cardin's design of the black chiffon dress that concealed the dancer's slack underarms while giving her great freedom of movement.

Geneva broke the silence when the ballet ended, "She was born in 1925 or '26. That makes her at least 55. She carries her years amazingly, don't you think?" She asked as she wrote *pride and defiance of time* in her notebook.

"Still busy scribbling," he whispered.

"Does it affect your concentration?"

"A little. I'd like to think you were really here beside me."

Geneva pulled her arm from the armrest between them.

"Albert, come out with it. What are you accusing me of, and why? You live with Anna, a woman you love. I have my work. It's what I do."

"Geneva, I need us to have good karma with one another."

"You're too metaphysical. Good karma is just a phrase, a cliché, to me."

Geneva looked down at the program again. Plisetskaya was dancing another surprise, scenes from *Carmen* by Roland Petit that Plisetskaya had never been allowed to perform in the U.S.S.R. because of its sexual explicitness.

Plisetskaya came flying on stage in red and black, whipping her ruffled skirts, a Firebird, a vamp who wielded her fan like Odile the Black Swan, whose every move was intended for conquest. Geneva surreptitiously scribbled under her sleeve *From Dying Swan to Anna, to Carmen, Maya Plisetskaya, fifty plus, eternal*, and felt consoled herself.

After the performance, they walked in silence across the campus onto Telegraph Avenue where young people crowded the sidewalk playing music and dirty children who looked as if they'd come with a gypsy clan begged money from them. She was glad when Albert chose a small Russian restaurant that got them off the avenue.

"How was your ice princess, your heroine, Natasha?" he asked.

"Not ice, no reproaches at all. Her husband looks out of Madame Tussaud's. The house is a museum of treasures on the Marina. Let's toast to good vibes, I can do that."

"Here's to missing and found persons!" He lifted his glass.

They drank. When he reached across to hold hands, she didn't pull away. "We've truly been friends, haven't we?" he asked. "We'll never not be friends."

"You keep changing. I'm the one who seems to just get older while you re-invent."

"You'll see I can be a friend. Anna and I will track the sister you spoke of."

"You've jumped ahead of me, but if she exists, which I don't have evidence for, I'll be so grateful. You can't wait forever—remember the last scene in *Dr. Zhivago*, the one where the older Zhivago, his heart worn out, arrives in Moscow. He's sitting on a tram when he sees a girl carrying a balalaika. Before he can get off the tram or call to her, he has a heart attack. It's the tragedy of missed timing. Remember that? She's carrying a balalaika. She's

Yuri and Lara's daughter but she'll never know they were that close."

"The meaning I take from it," he said, "is that you should pursue what you want and not wait. If such a person exists, try to find her. If not, what's been lost? You will have walked in Ruth's footsteps and maybe set the course of your life differently."

She reached across the table. "You do know me. Few people do."

"I'm not ready to say goodnight," he said when he paid the bill.

"We can walk to the Durant Hotel, just a few blocks."

Inside her small room, without words from either of them, they lay together on her single bed holding each other. For now, she thought, this is only for now. Their bodies fit as they had before so warmly and so easily it seemed to Geneva no violation to Anna, nor to herself, that they made deep and lingering love, years folded up like two people wrapped around each other.

———————

When Geneva woke up, she remembered Albert's words as he was getting dressed to go. "It doesn't matter you have a doubting nature. The universe connects us."

On the campus again, she showed her permission slip to watch the Bolshoi company practice in the Berkeley dance studio. The half dozen Russian men, solid and muscular, talked with the pretty, slim girls in black leotards. The dancers made funny faces and giggled at everything the boys said. Even the men on the sidelines, obvious KGB minders in big-shouldered suits, smoked and looked relaxed. Plisetskaya entered in a long-sleeved green leotard and matching tights. The morning light showed the lines around her mouth and hazel green eyes. A large mole near her lips moved as she breathed. Her deep red hennaed hair frizzed around a rubber band.

When the accompanist began, Plisetskaya strolled to her place at the barre, extended both arms and wrists, stretching her body in each position until perspiration rings spread under her arms and tendrils of sweaty curls stuck to her neck. She gave the warm-up exercises a Spanish flair as the accompanist played a refrain from Bizet. With her slanted and haughty aquiline nose, she still inhabited Carmen.

As she led men and women at the diagonal across the floor, Plisetskaya launched her straight body and aquiline nose through space, daring the younger dancers to match her elevation. She rose *en pointe* into a high arabesque stretching her neck.

"The splendor and genius amid the ordinary." Geneva recalled the words Andre Vosnesensky had written about Maya Plisetskaya. *The powerful goddess of dance*, Geneva wrote, *who wipes her nose with a rag and blows it hard.* The ballerina stayed a long while beside a dark young man with slanted Tatar eyes who Geneva recognized as the José to Plisetskaya's Carmen. Between the older woman and the youth ran a sexual current as clearly as if they'd been naked and just risen from bed. Geneva thought of Ruth's Tatar, of herself and Albert.

Twelve

In 1948, George Balanchine invited Jerome Robbins to join the New York City Ballet. Between them, the two geniuses of modern ballet in America had many muses over the years. Balanchine said of his Don Quixote, (1965, music by Nicolas Nabokov) one of very few story book ballets the Russian master put on stage, that it was about a man searching for his ideal, his muse and his love. Young and beautiful Suzanne Farrell was both. Jerome Robbins chose Natalia Makarova as his muse for Other Dances in 1976. Her partner was Mikhail Baryshnikov, a dancer in demand from the moment he defected. For 19 minutes, including applause and bows, the two former Kirov stars, dressed in muted rusts and browns, danced with perfect musicality and form, a marriage of the classical Russian ballet training with American innovation, and gave Natalia Makarova the ballet she yearned for.

Two years after she returned from California, Geneva was on her way to the Ballet Company Bookstore to look for back issues of *Icarus*. On the way, she bought two dozen pink tulips from a flower stand at 72nd and had them wrapped in tissue and pink cellophane. Since their final issue, *Icarus 21st Century*, had become a collectors' item, and Geneva wanted to make sure Connor had copies for the archives.

Before she reached 66th, Geneva watched a girl twirling a hula hoop and boys in the park flying kites. The anti-war demonstrations of a few years earlier were over and the feeling of a peaceful spring was in the air. Her eyes followed transparent ruffles and cream puff clouds reflected in the fountain at Lincoln Center before she walked across the plaza to the box office to read the casts for the upcoming 1983 ABT season. Russians were everywhere now that the U.S.S.R. seemed resigned to letting them go. Katya K, it turned out, was an East German. He'd had showed up in New York under his real name, Karl Klugman, before Ballets Trocaderos dubbed him Ekaterina "Kitty" Kitova. If *Icarus* were still in print, someone might have written an interesting story.

The owner of the bookshop stood on a ladder washing his windows.

"You look very Puckish in that green vest, George," Geneva said. George made her think of Connor, as if wearing matte makeup and rouge actually concealed wrinkles.

"You, my dear," George said, "have arrived by intuition at the appointed hour. And I see you brought our diva a bouquet. How sweet."

"What appointed hour? These are for Connor. I'm hoping you've got some back issues of *Icarus*. He'd come but he's not so well."

"I do know and wish him the best for me." George, who was at least 75, climbed down backwards to the sidewalk. "Natalia Makarova is coming into the shop to buy a rare Pavlova poster I've found for her."

"You mean we'll see Makarova this morning?"

"In New York, we live among legends. Do you still retain memories of that dreadful night in Paris?"

"I never wrote it up as such," Geneva said. "It went into my book, reflected in tranquility. I doubt it will make a ripple. I can't be hard on Nureyev any more."

"I agree. You're wise," he answered. "I hope that rumors of decline I've heard about Rudi are no more true than gossip surrounding him. He's one of a kind."

"Yes, he is, and I'm happy that Makarova is having so many opportunities—her own choreography, the revivals she's worked on, and now acting on Broadway! I shouldn't have worried about her. She's a triple threat."

"At the moment, audiences won't let Natasha out of their sight." George gave one last polish to the windows. "If you get advance copies of your new book, we'll have a warming party here, a Russian soiree."

"That would be wonderful, George. There's no more hallowed place than the Ballet Company. I'm not expecting *Russia's Rebellious Dancers* to sell as the children's storybooks did but my whole heart, my life, is in it. More new dancers jumping ship all the time—I couldn't keep up. I had to put an end to it. And finally, I'm going to Russia this summer with my aunt."

"If Natasha buys my Pavlova, I'm going to take a long vacation beside turquoise seas," he said. "Oh look, the lady comes."

Natalia Makarova emerged from a black car on the curve, followed by a second woman in a red coat, also wearing dark glasses, and then a muscular girl with pink hair carrying a camera and microphone. Makarova's small figure looked even more petite and delicate than Geneva remembered, her head wrapped in a gold scarf like a Nefertiti headdress. Immense dark glasses hid most of her face. With a swish of black silk clinging to her slim hips and high black boots, she strode ahead.

When Makarova removed her glasses and stepped forward to examine the portrait of Pavlova, George lifted the photograph so the camera got a good shot of the two Giselles facing each other across time.

He stage-whispered, "You can take it home, Madame Makarova."

"Very nice," said the ballerina. "Anna Palovna Pavlova, she is idol to me."

"Tell me about your favorite partners." The woman in her red coat held a WBAI mic close, daring, Geneva thought, to ask the questions she'd been wanting to ask.

"Oh, many! Don't ask favorite," Makarova laughed.

"You don't have a favorite?"

"Anthony Dowell, I love intensity. Ivan Nagy is generous partner. Misha Baryshnikov, great artist and tender in love scenes." Makarova's low voice carried.

"What about Nureyev?" the interviewer asked. "Now that Misha challenges him."

"Nureyev?" She frowned. "Not like others. True artist, difficult partner."

Without the dark glasses, Makarova's deep blue eyes and protruding teeth still dominated her face but the ballerina's cheek line appeared fuller.

"I would like picture sent to apartment," Makarova told George, who still held the poster of Pavlova as if she might return to life.

"We have been speaking with the prima ballerina *assoluta,* Natalia Makarova," said the woman with the mic. "Only once in a great while an *assoluta* is born. She is a mystery beyond technique and training, though she's got all that and more. Miss Makarova is of that select sisterhood, and now she takes Madame Pavlova home with her."

"Thank you. My most beautiful memory of Russia. I remain Russian in heart." Makarova placed her hand over her breast and walked toward her car.

"She's had face work in Paris," George whispered. "They make everyone look gamine, like Leslie Caron. Why didn't you give her the flowers or ask her a question about what she's dancing now?"

"The flowers are for Connor. I don't have more questions."

———————

It was a fine day for walking and Geneva entered the park at 72nd Street. Children and dogs were everywhere. When she reached Park Avenue and saw the ancient doorman before Connor's building, she thought that for his age, it was a miracle he was standing.

She rang upstairs. "Another day, my dear. Tomorrow perhaps," Connor said.

"I'll just leave you pretty tulips," she spoke into the phone.

Back in her apartment an hour later, she called Jeffrey. "Is he really ill?"

"He's been sleeping in the cassock the silent monks gave him," Jeffrey said.

"That sounds scratchy."

"There's more, he's been sleeping in a casket. He thanks you for the flowers."

"I feel left out and kept in the dark, Jeff. I haven't seen him since we took him to the airport last month. I thought it was a good sign he was traveling but he had so little luggage, and he accepted that wheelchair to the gate."

"He packed himself."

"Something you're hiding, Jeff. All that pancake makeup."

"He flirted with the wheelchair attendant." Jeff's voice rose. "'Hermes, come to take me to the gods,' he said. "Oh, hold on. The Master is up and coming to say hello."

"How is my dear Bacchus doing?" Connor asked.

"He's smiling more like a geisha every minute," she answered.

"Did you know that Caravaggio died younger than I am now? Under some brutish circumstances, a brawl, an infection, all very sordid."

"Connor! What a comparison. You're not going to get in a brawl."

"No, of course. We did bring beauty to their attention, didn't we?"

"*Icarus 21st Century*. They are almost impossible to buy now."

"I may come back. Don't count me out."
"I never will."

———————

Connor St. John, hereafter to be called Brother Christopher, has made application to join the Order. Our Brother will not be able to write nor speak directly to you for a certain time, but we will be happy to answer communication addressed to him. Through our secretary, Brother Christopher will be in touch concerning liquidation of certain works of art and other possessions.

Geneva looked at the cancellation on the stamp. *Big Sur, California.* Where was that? She wondered. She'd have to ask Albert.

"The monks cultivate healing herbs and keep bees," said Jeffrey.

"Wait a minute, you two. Ruth, please tell me why you and Jeff are in on this. I've been kept in the dark."

"You're not the only one surprised. He was always crazy about Jesuits' secret messages," Jeff said, "but a silent order of monks? Silence must be the worst penance for Connie."

Another envelope, *St. John's Testimony*, lay unopened on the desk.

"I will open now," said Ruth. "It is time."

Under the a Manhattan legal firm's letter head were typed instructions to sell St. John's French furniture, Persian carpets, Czech and Chinese porcelain, Steinways, the family silver, and all else moveable to pay his debts. Whatever remained was to be divided by Geneva, Ruth and Jeff. They were to call the attorney when sales were complete and distribution ready.

"I don't believe this." Geneva sat down. "He's alive and giving us everything. What will he live on?"

"Without Connie, I'd have gone home to Kansas long ago," Jeff said.

"Now you can you stay in New York," Geneva said. "If there's anything left of his estate after debts."

Jeff shook his head.

"You could live with us," said Geneva. "We could get a bigger apartment."

"That's so sweet, but my sister wants me to come home to help out in her ballet school. I'm no great talent but I can teach. Connor chose me from the chorus line of *Guys and Dolls.* Sent me flowers. I was happy enough to hang up my shoes and be taken care of. I've been happy. I will miss him so much. I'll miss you."

"Wait, we don't know," said Ruth. "He's only away."

"Did anyone get that stage set?" Jeff asked in a low voice.

"I never gave it back," said Geneva. "If we were to find a girl, maybe someone's granddaughter, who has *Swan Lake* in her future, I'll give it to her. Won't we do that Ruth, if we should find a missing person somewhere in Russia?"

Acknowledgments

The Dance Collection at the New York Public Library for the Performing Arts for the many videos and books I used there; Natalia Makarova, for granting me time and giving all of us her beauty; Dina Makarova who made access to the dancer possible; the memory of Rudolf Nureyev which continues to haunt stages and trouble authorities in Russia; Maya Plisetskaya for inspiration; The Covent Garden Opera House and New York State Theater for making standees welcome; University of California at Berkeley and the Bolshoi dancers for access to rehearsals and company classes. For friends, readers and helpers Michael Morey, Deanna Watt, Katherine Lench Meyering, John Schak, my PILS pals and editors, Marylu Downing, Susan Swartz and Robin Beeman. The publishers of many books about dance and dancers in America, Great Britain and Russia which I've read over the years. My gratitude to the receptive and enthusiastic publishers of Open Books, David Ross and Kelly Huddleston, for their creative work and their open minds.

Made in the USA
Middletown, DE
25 November 2017